DEATH IN
THE TRUFFLE WOOD

Also by Pierre Magnan

The Messengers of Death

DEATH IN
THE TRUFFLE WOOD

Pierre Magnan

Translated from the French by
Patricia Clancy

THOMAS DUNNE BOOKS
ST. MARTIN'S MINOTAUR
NEW YORK

This is a work of fiction. All of the characters, organizations, and events portrayed in this novel are either products of the author's imagination or are used fictitiously.

THOMAS DUNNE BOOKS.
An imprint of St. Martin's Press.

DEATH IN THE TRUFFLE WOOD. Copyright © 1978 by Pierre Magnan. English translation copyright © 2005 by Patricia Clancy. All rights reserved. Printed in the United States of America. For information, address St. Martin's Press, 175 Fifth Avenue, New York, N.Y. 10010.

www.thomasdunnebooks.com
www.minotaurbooks.com

Library of Congress Cataloging-in-Publication Data

Magnan, Pierre, 1922–
  [Commissaire dans la truffière. English]
  Death in the truffle wood / Pierre Magnan ; translated from the French by Patricia Clancy.—1st. St. Martin's Minotaur paperback ed.
      p. cm.
  ISBN-13: 978-0-312-36719-0
  ISBN-10: 0-312-36719-8
  I. Clancy, P. A. II. Title.

PQ2625.A637 C613 2007
843'.914—dc22

2007014867

First published as *La commissaire dans la truffière* in France by Librairie Arthème Fayard

First St. Martin's Minotaur Paperback Edition: September 2008

10 9 8 7 6 5 4 3 2 1

For my friend
Maurice Chevaly

I

"COME ON ROSELINE! JUST ONE MORE? DIG ME UP ANOTHER one!"

Lying on his side with his head resting on his hand and a blade of grass dangling from his lips, Alyre Morelon was stroking Roseline with words as well as gestures. And Roseline was giving little grunts of satisfaction while affectionately licking his beard with her tongue, which smelled deliciously of fresh truffles.

"Come on Roseline. Don't be silly. Just one. Get me one more and then we'll go home."

But Roseline needed a lot of coaxing. She kept giving him gentle persuasive head butts, obviously meaning, "Get going! It's time to go home. You've got enough for today. Your eyes are bigger than your stomach."

Alyre looked at his basket and sighed. It contained scarcely four kilos and the agent had ordered ten for Saturday.

"You're a lazy lump!" he said. "I'm not speaking to you any more."

He turned over on to his other side. Then it was Roseline who gave her equivalent of a sigh. She ferreted about a bit at the base of the truffle tree with the twisty trunk. An almond tree with a trunk twisted as though it had been wrung by the strong hands of a washerwoman was a fairly rare occurrence in a truffle wood of young oaks. In this area of the Basses-Alpes you do sometimes come across these myst- erious tree trunks rising up in a rigid spiral around their axis as if the sky were drawing them up.

Truffles are unpredictable things. You think you'll find one at the base of a strong young tree in well-raked ground. But no. It's there waiting for you under the tangled brush of a gnarled juniper bush or under a 200-year-old oak, where supposedly nobody has ever found a single one before. It's waiting for you . . . It sits there waiting for you when you have a Roseline to help you.

"Cro!"

It was *the* cry, an inimitable cry, or rather a kind of short click. Alyre reached her with one bound, bent over and took the truffle to the basket. It could not have been far short of fifty grams.

"Oh! It's a beauty! Yes indeed, that's a real beauty, Madame!"

He knelt down close to her and kissed the sow twice on her silky fat cheeks. She was so happy to please him that she wagged her rump, knocking him down and sending both of them rolling, clinging to each other amid a chorus of grunts and giggles, over that blessed ground, half-air, half-earth, which was their gold mine.

"Roseline, you silly cow! Watch what you're doing. You're squashing me."

He got to his feet and picked up the basket. In the distance a smell of soup wafted on the air. It was time. Smoke was drifting down from the village, a sign that he should come home.

Walking one behind the other, they reached the edge of the oak woods. The empty white road rose up towards Banon.

"Wait a minute, Roseline. I'll have to put your collar on again because of the cars . . ."

The collar was actually a pink ribbon that originally came from the big chocolate bell that Alyre had given his son for his eighth birthday. Like Alyre, this son adored Roseline, who earned at least half the cost of his studies in Paris. One day he took the ribbon, which the flies loved to buzz around, from the mirror in his bedroom where it had been draped for years, saying to his father, "Here. Put it around her neck . . . until I see her again."

This collar attached to a piece of old string was strictly for show as Roseline, who was probably aware of her commercial value, never wandered from the side of the road. Never . . . And yet, since last summer she had sometimes taken it into her head to make a sudden dash through the oaks or run directly for the cover of the laurels. As a matter of fact, that very evening . . .

"Roseline! What's got into you? What are you doing?"

With one quick jerk, she had just pulled the string right out of his hand. Off she went towards that mass of liquid bronze, shimmering in the evening wind and clicking like the lances of an army on the move. It was a large grove of laurel trees. They had suffered badly twenty years ago in the great frost. Some had sprouted again from the base; others from the dead branches. All this regrowth reached straight for the sky, stiff as broomsticks, shaking the dismal bells of their poisonous fruit.

Alyre caught up with Roseline at the edge of the thicket. He stopped there for a moment. He felt, as he did every time that he lingered at the edge of the laurel grove, that there was something in the air, some new oddness about the place. He had the impression that a big dark car was hiding deep in the wood. But what would it be doing there away from any of the roads nearby? And besides, if you worried about everything you saw . . .

They set off again, one pulling the other, and both of them grumbling. Alyre picked up the basket of truffles he had left on the dry grass on the slope. In front of the wall of laurels he raised his basket to breathe in the earthy smell and dispel the unpleasant feeling that had spoiled his good mood. He had been hunting truffles for more than forty years but he could never have enough of that aroma.

He never sold the first ones of the season. Despite Francine's cries of protest, he kept them for three days in an airtight jar with six eggs taken straight from the nest. The truffles exuded their odour through the pores of the shell into the white and the yolk of the eggs. A subtle exchange took place between them until they combined to create something new and different. When the runny omelette appeared on the table one windy evening, as the stove with its bubbling kettle warmed your back, it was an absolute feast of taste and smell.

Roseline trotted along the edge of the road in the dust of that dry late afternoon in November. Now Roseline was the only sow in the district that was likely to die of old age. Her huge thighs would never be rubbed with salt to be cured with saltpetre and turned into hams. Her fat would never be melted down into lard. Roseline was one of those rarest of females that dug up truffles without eating them, except of course when she was given one as a reward. Even then you had to be prudent for fear of destroying her sense of smell, for just as a drunkard will never be able to tell a Château Latour from a Château Haut-Brion, Roseline would soon lose the ability to detect truffles in the soil if she were given too many.

With her head set off by the pink ribbon, Roseline trots towards the sty where the bran and potato mash awaits her, nice and hot, and smelling of the summer harvest. The delight of every pig in the world.

II

THE CARRIAGE ENTRANCE LED INTO A SQUARE COURTYARD. On one side were the hens and to the south of them, the rabbit cages. A smell of crushed grass floated in the air under the rafters of the sheepfold, warmed by the flock inside. The room was on the first floor under the roof of the covered terrace, supported by a square pillar.

With his basket on his arm, Alyre scraped his shoes on the mounting block and stepped lightly up the outside staircase. He pulled the fly-wire door towards him, then opened the glass door.

Francine was taking the onion soup, with its bread and cheese crust, out of the oven. The table was set around the dark red wine, part-Alicante, part-Jacquez, that prohibited variety of grape. But it came from very old vines and Francine was deputy mayor. A blind eye was turned to these plantings that should have been pulled out ages ago.

The shepherd was already sitting at the table, clutching his knife and fork with point and prongs in the air as is right and proper. Everything about his squat frame proclaimed, "Well, where is it?" The three dogs under the table were getting ready to snap up the scraps from the feast.

"Just look at him over there! He wouldn't give me a hand if you paid him." Francine waved a dismissive hand in his direction.

"You told me that I was too clumsy."

5

"Oh, that's true enough!"

The shepherd was Pascal, the only son of a reasonably well-off family, who had turned his back on them all because his mother was deceiving his father. He had left home without a word, keeping the secret to himself. He was nineteen. Nearly every Saturday his mother would come and pester him even when he was in the fields where the sheep were grazing.

"But why? Why? You had free bed and board at home! Your father and I waited on you hand and foot!" Pascal's back was still turned to her as she spoke. He never replied, but just went on with his work. He said "Hello Ma" when she arrived and "Goodbye Ma" when she left.

"To think that there are people," Alyre remarked, "who would actually go down on their knees to be told a few home truths! But you'll see. One of these days, he'll give her the truth. Right to her face! And then we'll have to go and pick her up in the field where he's let her fall! In a dead faint. Flat on her face in the goat shit!"

Francine always turned away when Alyre said that fine word, the truth. What on earth would he know about the truth, when she had been lying to him for twelve years, without him saying a thing?

She glanced at the basket on the floor.

"Is that all you've brought back? You didn't exactly strain yourselves, you two, did you?"

Actually, there was more than 1000 francs' worth. And that would continue from 15 November until 15 February, apart from any interruptions due to bad weather. There was really nothing to complain about, but Francine's tactic was to appear as bad tempered as before.

Alyre always felt the same pleasure when he gazed at her.

"Just look at her with her fancy things," he would say to himself. "Isn't she gorgeous? How that woman loves jewellery! The wristwatch covered with precious stones. The necklace of artificial pearls and the ring with a stone big enough to choke a horse. How it all sparkles. How it gleams! More than if it wasn't fake. It's unbelievable what they manage to do these days!"

And it was true that Francine's jewels – her only weakness – did

6

shine under the light hanging from the ceiling and gave the place a festive air. She put them on every day with great care after she had finished the chores. "She loves them," people said. "That Francine really loves jewellery."

Slim and erect, Francine, now forty-one, always dressed in dark colours so that nothing got really dirty. At first sight she seemed fairly lacking in love and only good enough for one man. But a surprise was in store for any man who touched her, by chance or by design. She was supple and firm, and her flat belly was as hard as an athlete's. You felt that it was capable of unexpectedly exciting movements.

It was politics that brought this to the fore. Until she was thirty, she belonged to that generation of women who resigned themselves to whatever kind of love fell to their lot. But when she was elected to the town council, then to deputy mayor, she got to know people during those moments when the councillors relaxed after various meetings. One day a councillor from another commune got her up to dance for fun. That samba took his breath away.

"My God, Francine!" he said to her, "I'm sorry, but you're a bit too hot for me."

From that day on, she began to dance at the parties that were held after conferences or union meetings. And then, inevitably, she also began to indulge in the rest, but not without sighs and hesitation. She hated the complications and lies involved, so she introduced her lovers to Alyre.

"Alyre! Tomorrow I'm going to Les Angles with Monsieur Maucœur. We've been appointed to check the second stage of the work being done on the water supply . . . You'll find everything prepared in the fridge."

"Alyre, this is Dr Malgriaux, from the Public Health Department . . . I've been asked to show him around the children's holiday camps in the canton, etc . . ."

If ever the opposition won the municipal elections, Francine would either have to kill herself or tell the truth.

"The truth," thought Alyre, as he ate his onion soup. "As if I didn't know the truth."

But for him, as long as he had Roseline, the truffles and the bees, well the rest . . .

"The soup's not thick enough!" Francine exclaimed.

No-one bothered to comment. Alyre was hungry and he'd eat it however it was.

As for the shepherd . . . His spoon had stopped half-way between the plate and his open mouth, as he followed the progress of something on the wall, something seen only by him, some insubstantial presence that had suddenly flown out of the clock case. Now it seemed to be gliding swiftly over the kitchen utensils; then it turned the corner of the mantelpiece, leaving a trace of its dust on each of the spice tins: Sugar, Salt, Pepper, Cinnamon. It clouded up the mantle of the kerosene lamp and finally disappeared down the plug hole of the chrome steel sink, taking the shepherd's gaze with it.

"Will you look at him!" exclaimed Francine, who had been observing him. "What do you think he's seen this time? He looks like a cat watching a ghost."

And that's what he was doing. Beneath his mop of long hair, the eyes of the nineteen-year-old shepherd were as large as those of a Romanesque Christ, so dark, so deep, and it was indeed a ghost that they were following from the clock to the sink. Like cats, he had the gift.

"It's enough to make your blood boil!" Francine said.

She was always afraid that, some way or another, her secrets would surface. And it occurred to her that a ghost could well be the means of that happening.

It took a while for the shepherd to come down to earth. It took a while for him to recognise Francine whom he loved in vain and in all humility.

"Another one has disappeared," he said in a low, muffled voice.

"Another what?" Francine exclaimed.

She thought that he had lost a lamb and didn't dare own up.

"I don't know . . . It's the gendarmes. I was looking after the sheep at La Charitonne . . ."

"On the road to Montsalier?"

"Yes, the one that goes through the Le Deffens woods."

"And . . . ?"

"And they got out of their van to ask me if I had seen him."

"But who are you talking about?"

"Someone who has disappeared."

"What was his name?"

"Jeremy . . ."

"Well, that's a great help!"

"That's what I said to the gendarmes, but they asked me again. So I said, 'What does this Jeremy look like?' Then they described him to me: 'A brown robe with white bands made in Indonesia by a Buddhist colony,' they said. 'Noisy Swedish clogs. Long hair and wooden beads with a book pendant hanging around his neck beneath his beard.' That's what the gendarmes said. 'Oh, and we forgot! He also had a big mandolin on a strap across his chest.' Believe it or not, since the beginning of the season I've seen maybe sixty of them going up there towards Montsalier. And they're all like you say."

"All of them!" said Francine. "One passed this way three days ago and wanted me to give him an egg. Giraud's wife over at Les Parmelles told me a bit about how they live. They've put tarpaulins over the collapsed roof of the old church. They do their cooking around the font filled with rainwater. And they've burnt all the pews that were still there."

The shepherd went on, "'Since you have long hair too,' the policemen said to me, 'we thought that perhaps you were a bit friendly with them. They've come from Noyers-sur-Jabron. Does that mean anything to you, Noyers-sur-Jabron?' And they looked at me like gendarmes do when they're suspicious of someone."

He stopped speaking. The wind was rustling through the elder tree under the balcony. It brought a whiff of the sheepfold to them in gusts. The ram's bell tinkled as he changed position. The shepherd listened to it. He was drawing another ghost from the clock case, following it the length of the chimney piece, and off over to the modern sink where it disappeared in a long spiral.

9

"That's the fourth since September," the shepherd said. "The fourth that the gendarmes have questioned me about like that . . ."

"Indeed?" Alyre said, ". . . And by the way, while we're on the subject, Francine, there's something strange about these goings-on, don't you think? . . . Do you think that can happen . . . ? Do you think that it's possible for . . . ?"

He carefully wound a long string of grated cheese around his spoon, swallowed it and wiped his mouth. Then he reached for his glass of dark red wine, which he raised to the light. No doubt about it. Light just doesn't penetrate Jacquez wine . . .

While he was pondering the possible endings to his sentence, he was unaware that the shepherd was sitting there expectantly with his spoon still midway between the plate and his half-open mouth. And Francine too was waiting for him to end his sentence with a full ladle in her hand.

Finally, she burst out, "What? What can't happen? What's strange? Spit it out, for heaven's sake! You're maddening, the both of you: one tracks ghosts as if they were flies, and the other loses the thread when he starts to speak. Tell me! Explain yourself! Say what you mean!"

The shepherd's eyes were wide-open and shining with eagerness. Not only did he anticipate the worst, but he was always happy at the prospect.

"Oh!" said Alyre, whose opening remarks had just convinced him not to say anything further. "Oh! . . . It's something you'd need to know everything about before you could understand it. Everything! And as we know nothing . . ."

His mind was preoccupied with sombre thoughts of what could be happening down there near the Cassagne truffle woods, among the bronze spears of the branches in the laurel thicket. Did that army of lances ever stop clicking in the night wind? Those mad dashes that Roseline had been making for some time now, just when she went by that wood – you'd have to admit, they were strange. And that hot, stifling feeling he got now when he was listening to the sounds in the air on the edge of that wood as he attached the string to Roseline's ribbon – you'd have to admit, they were strange too.

"I can't believe this," Francine said. "I'm not used to you being so mysterious!"

"It's not about being mysterious," Alyre said, "It's about being puzzled. Yes, that's it. I'm puzzled . . ."

This puzzlement drove him to seek more general company that evening. As soon as they had finished the cheese, he got up, put his table napkin into the ring engraved with his name, and announced that he was going out to play cards at Rosemonde Burle's place.

III

THE CLOCK ON THE DASHBOARD COULD BE HEARD TICKING
in the gloom. The big blue car was deep in the wood, under the cover
of the laurel trees. The wind sometimes blew down a dark fruit, which
ricocheted on the roof. The only thing that could be seen through the
windscreen was the white patch of two tense hands, lit up by a ray of
moonlight filtering through the waving branches.

"Is that your last word?"

The girl with the hands gripping the steering wheel was staring
straight ahead. Her bright eyes were misty with tears, and the sobs that
rose in her throat made it hard for her to speak.

"Anyone would think that this was a love scene, a lovers' quarrel . . ."

The man beside her had a bushy beard and long hair falling in dread-
locks. He answered her in a sombre voice, also staring straight ahead
at an old crumbling wall with an iron gate.

"Anyone would think that this *is* a love scene . . ."

"No, it isn't! It's a quarrel over money!"

"10,000,000 francs!* You're going to give these down-and-outs
10,000,000! And you try to tell me that it's not love! The half of

* 667,000 euros, or £460,512, in today's currency.

12

everything we own! Just think about it! The sweat of two generations built that!"

"Yes, the sweat of two generations of profiteers!"

"But what are you trying to prove by doing this?"

"It's atonement. I'm atoning for my father, for my mother, and for you incidentally . . . Just listen to me. In forty, fifty years you'll be old or dead. You'll have had a husband you no longer love, children who wonder what to do with you because they don't dare push you downstairs . . . yet. You'll have seen them get ugly as they grow older. The God you've been raised to worship won't be any use to you then. And your whole life won't ever have been any use because you'll have loved nothing outside of your little family unit. And what's really awful in your case, is that you'll keep on loving them even though they're revolting."

"Why would they be revolting?"

"Because parents like ours, who never talked about anything but money, can only have dreadful children. And you'll choose a husband, as if by chance, from among other dreadful children!"

"Father gave to charity!"

The man sneered.

"Correct! He made such a show of his donations that people always thought he was sharing his fortune. No, it can't go on! I must escape from all that! I can't bear to be like that! I don't want to be tainted by it. Everyone in the world should be brothers. I couldn't take my place among men if I was like that. If I was like you."

He looked as if he was about to open the car door.

"No! Wait!" she said breathlessly. "I can go to 6,000,000. You know it's my whole life, that I studied for it, that I've given it everything I've got!"

"You're a boss, heart and soul!" he said scornfully. "How is that possible? How can *you* be like that? You used to rush to give your dolls to all the poor girls in Oyonnax."

"And I was rapped over the knuckles for it!"

"Not by our parents! There was no chance of them doing that. They had one of the maids give you a stern lecture about not sharing things. When did you stop sharing? When did you stop giving? Tell me! Can't you go back to being as you were? Can't you start to be like me again? I was so fond of you."

"You love me but you're trying to screw 4,000,000 out of me!"

"I've got all the quotes. I've found out all the possible discounts: the purchase of all the land, all the ruins, restoration of the houses, laying on the water, electricity etc. To house the community in a beautiful natural setting, I'll need all of it."

"All of it! You're mad!"

"You know that's not true. I have three maths certificates. And you've had me secretly put under observation twice. Yes you have! It's no use protesting. I know that your love is . . ."

"The Europlast Group has its eye on us. They've made sure that no-one else can outbid them. It could well be that you won't even get the six million I'm offering you."

The man in the shadows gave a slight smile.

"You'll always outwit me, but all the same I'm not so stupid as to believe that. I know that you've had a professional assessment done by an American group. I've also had a bit of commercial espionage done on you by a friend of mine who is a private detective. The factory has been valued at 25,000,000, and 20,000,000 is the top figure Europlast has set for the gamble to be profitable. Don't forget that they'll shut down the factory as soon as they buy it. All they'll take is the list of clients. And so little sister . . . 10,000,000 is my last offer!"

He opened the car door, and this time without any hesitation. He was immediately aware of an unpleasant smell. His eyes wandered up into the laurel branches. The clouds were scudding past the moon.

"Jeremy!"

She had slammed her door and walked around the car to bar his way.

"You're crucifying me!"

The moon lit up her whole figure in the hand-woven woollen coat: her hair blowing in the wind, her legs in their sheer stockings and the high-heeled shoes that shone when the moonlight hit them. She was a young woman with clear skin and huge eyes. Her face was full of kindness and intelligence.

"How beautiful you are!" Jeremy murmured. "What a shame! How can you put up with that pathetic lot? Your husband will look at the World Cup on TV. He'll take you to see real porno films on business dinner evenings. You'll cook dead lambs on barbecues! You'll have a life that's ordinary in the extreme. Come with me. Here in the hills you'll meet men from everywhere. They may be dirty on the outside but at least they're clean on the inside. You'll know several of them, freely and without constraint, until you find the right man . . . or woman. Who knows? But at least in our world you'll be free to choose."

"Jeremy! I beg you! Without the factory, I'm nothing, just an empty shell. Please accept my offer. I swear to you that if I could do more I would."

Jeremy turned round to confront her. Framed by its shaggy hair, his face had the same tender expression as the young woman's.

"My God . . ." he groaned, "how can you hide all that under such an innocent exterior? How can you be like that and so naïve at the same time?"

All her energy seemed to disappear. She no longer reacted to his words. Where was he now, the brother she had loved, who was one of them? Where was his heart? Where was his soul? She was suddenly overcome by a long-suppressed urge to pray. But he was turning away, about to leave . . .

She watched him set off, taking her last hope with him. The factory would be sold. She couldn't give him 10,000,000. The sacred Swiss bank account couldn't be touched. Her father had made her swear it. Only if the family had to flee France could it ever be used.

"Jeremy!"

He was leaving, barefoot, with his thin shabby robe gathered around him like a monk's, but poorer still without belt or crucifix, except for the clicking wooden beads.

"God!" she thought, "How cold he must be."

Her eye was caught by the white wheel trims on her luxury car glowing in the moonlight. The right front tyre was flat.

"Jeremy!" she called.

He turned and came back.

"Jeremy! I've never changed a tyre in my life. It would happen today of all days . . ."

He shrugged. "Do you have any tools?"

"In the boot."

He got busy, jacked up the car and took out the spare wheel.

"Doesn't it hurt your feet going without shoes like that?"

"Of course not! I'm proud of my hard skin. I've walked 5000 kilometres barefoot. They don't wear out like tyres, you know. Shit! They've screwed on the nuts too tightly. Those mechanics are all the same! They tighten them with a wheel brace, and all you've got is this silly tubular thing. Stupid bastards, the lot of them! Would you have an adjustable spanner? I'll put it through the tube for leverage."

He searched around in the tool box, then came back. He carefully placed the nuts in the hubcaps. He changed the wheel, screwing the nuts back on by hand.

"Here, hold this for me."

He handed her the heavy spanner which he had used as a lever. He was bent over in front of her, the crown of his hairy head level with the bonnet.

She was thinking, "10,000,000. And my future . . . What will I do?"

It was all the descendants of the family, living and dead, who raised the spanner in the young woman's arm and brought it down with all her strength on Jeremy's head. Once, twice . . .

She was suddenly gripped by an overwhelming fear, for instead of falling, he began to straighten up, slowly, slowly, just as he had raised the car with the jack. She realised then that if he turned round, without him even doing anything, she would surely die too, of horror, regret, dismay . . . Then she struck him a third time with the force of despair, and this time he collapsed against the bonnet. But the last picture she would keep of him was not this tall sagging body in its robe, but the man still alive as he rose up so incredibly slowly; the man who was about to show her his face, she knew it, the face of someone who now knew her as she really was!

"I killed him because he was right," she said to herself. But that admission was immediately pushed aside by the thought that she was the link between the past and the future. What did it matter that she had committed murder? By killing Jeremy she was saving a whole enterprise and all its workers. "And you save yourself," a voice cried to her. Suddenly, what she had been before that moment rose to the surface of her mind again. Had she really been capable of doing such a thing?

She looked at her arm as if it belonged to somebody else; she stared at the spanner sticky with blood. She threw it away. The noise it made as it hit the ground revived her instinct. She had to cover her tracks, leave, get away . . . She picked up the spanner, bent down to finish tightening the wheel nuts and replace the hubcap. During this whole operation as she was bending over the wheel, her pure, smooth face was on a level with Jeremy's, and her long hair mingled with his.

She stood up at last, dragged the wheel over to the boot, put it in and went round the car to the driver's seat. She must get away . . . No-one knew that she had left Oyonnax to come here to Banon. No-one. She had filled up with petrol the day before. She hadn't even had to stop at a service station. If she could leave straight away and get back to Oyonnax before daybreak, who would suspect her? Who would see through the grief she would feel and properly show in public? Only Jeremy's lawyer knew he intended to sell the factory. If Jeremy hadn't expressly told her about it this evening, even she would still have known nothing about it. Everything pointed to her getting out of all this with clean hands.

She looked at her watch. It was half past midnight. Five hours driving at 150 kms an hour . . . It could be done. She put out her hand to open the car door. Then she saw Mambo. A tiny dachshund was standing on its short back legs and leaning its front paws against the closed window. It looked at her, whimpering, anxious to get back to its master. She recoiled at the sight of it. Once again she had the image of her brother, happy and friendly, walking on the road with his little dog in his arms and a big tramp's bag hanging around his neck. The bag was still there too. Perhaps it still had the smell of Jeremy's sweat as he walked the roads . . .

Oh no! She covered her face with her hands. She had been able to kill because the factory demanded it. She couldn't kill the dachshund. That was more than she was capable of. She would lose him . . . somewhere along the way . . . He was a pedigree dog. Someone would pick him up and give him a home . . .

IV

AS SHE WAS ABOUT TO GET BEHIND THE WHEEL, SHE HEARD an old car bumping over the dirt track towards her. It was advancing slowly, shaken this way and that by the ruts, its patched-up bumper bar rattling like pots and pans. Who could possibly be coming to such a deserted spot at this hour? In front of the Mercedes there was a wooded hollow deeply shaded by thick foliage. She got behind the wheel, turned on the ignition, backed a few metres then drove forward into the dell until she could hear the branches whipping against the body of the car. She did all that without turning on the headlights. She got out, took cover among the laurel trees and stood straight and white in the moon-light. The curtain of trees screened her from the clearing strewn with dead leaves in front of the wall with its rusty iron gate.

This dense thicket, which she had noticed from the road after she had picked up Jeremy from their meeting-place at the crossroads, had looked like a suitable place for a private conversation. At that moment and without her being aware of it, fate was no doubt already suggesting to her that she would probably have to kill him. But now she was a prisoner of the thicket. There was no other way to get out to the road than by that dirt track where the old car was coming towards her. It was chugging closer, but oh so slowly. You could hear the sound of its wheezy engine labouring in second gear. It was wheezy but it was also solid, and you felt it could last for another twenty years at this snail's pace. This car was also being driven through the narrow track overgrown with laurel branches with all its lights off. At last it appeared, entering the clearing in the dappled moonlight playing in the wind through the laurels and holly-oaks.

The bodywork had once been white, but now it was cracked and grey like a tortoise's shell, so old and worn by being left in the open for years that it hardly seemed of this world. A sinister aura played around the old jalopy. Standing there, stiff with fear and foreboding, she looked at it and her blood ran cold. If the driver turned on his lights, he couldn't miss seeing Jeremy's body lying in a heap on the dead leaves. But why were all his lights off? What was he doing here at this hour in this garden shut off by an iron gate?

The engine cut out suddenly. In the silence that enveloped everything once more, the young woman heard a tall tree begin to moan softly in the wind. The sound rose very slowly and seemed to her like the dismal sough of a cypress. She was staring as hard as she could at the grey car standing motionless in the gloom, its windows misted up in the December cold, when she heard the door creak. The driver's seat was facing in the opposite direction to the thicket of holly-oaks where she was hiding. She didn't see him until he stood up, with his back turned to her. He walked nonchalantly towards the rusty gate. Despite the moonlight, his silhouette was vague, stiff and black from head to toe, without waist, shoulders or neck. He stopped at the gate and took out a bunch of rattling keys. There was the sound of a well-oiled lock turning effortlessly. The gate creaked on its hinges as the man pushed it wide open. Then he turned round.

The young woman saw him full length, all black apart from patches of shadow and moonlight – a shapeless scarecrow without a face. A black net veil hung from the huge brim of his black hat and bunched out over his shoulders and arms down to the elbows. He wore long black gloves that looked like women's gloves.

She stood there transfixed, looking at him through holes in the foliage.

The dead leaves crunched underfoot as he went back to the old car. But he suddenly stopped before reaching it, legs together, arms close to his body, standing still like a hunter who wants to blend into the foliage. She held her breath. They were only twenty metres from each other. Earlier, in the car, she had smoked a cigarette, and she could smell the subtle perfume she used in the air around her. It could have given her away had there not been that acrid smell floating beneath the trees which dominated everything else. Nevertheless, the man standing stiff and tense slowly turned the deathly dark curtain hiding his face first to one side then to the other, and his hat followed its movement. He began walking towards his car again, even more slowly. He seemed to be hesitant, as if working something out. If he suddenly took it into his head to brush past the laurels and proceed towards the first sheltering clump of holly-oaks, he would most certainly discover Jeremy's body and then . . . she would never have time to get away.

Even though he still looked extremely wary, he kept walking in the same direction. Only once did he suddenly turn round. It was when the rusty gate, which was probably bent on its hinges, was pushed back slightly by the wind with a loud creak that seemed to worry the cautious man. He stood gazing at the dark opening cut across by a single moonbeam. Then, no doubt reassured, he began walking again.

He didn't go back to the driver's seat. He opened the rear door on the opposite side from where she was watching him. With some difficulty he pulled out a kind of floppy, oblong puppet, which seemed to slip into his arms. He had all the trouble in the world holding on to it, tottering as he heaved it up. He stood up straight again and slowly lumbered towards the open gate.

It was then that the moonlight suddenly revealed what the man was carrying on his shoulders. It looked just like Jeremy's body, yet she could still see it where she had left it, lying in the grass. She was stunned. Shivers went down her spine and made her scalp tingle as though she had received an electric shock. The beads, the robe, the feet which the stranger was holding by the ankles: they were all there, everything was the same. The hair on his head almost swept the ground, hiding his face. The shadowy figure was already slipping through the gateway and disappearing inside. The young woman couldn't move. She knew that Jeremy's body was still there . . . Well then, who was the person being carried by the man in the veil? Why was he dead? What did the man intend doing with him? The desire to find out drove her forward. She followed him through the gate.

When the man returned, he didn't turn round straight away. First he pulled the creaky gate towards him and double-locked it. Then he came back towards his car with the same slow deliberate steps as before. Then he raised his head. There in the shadows, a young woman's face was watching him intently. He could hardly believe his eyes. His first reaction was fear, but the face was so inviting that he was quickly reassured. There was nothing to fear from such an open expression. Unfortunately he didn't have any of the necessary with him . . . He looked at his hands, and to show his confidence, spat in them.

He approached slowly. He pulled back the laurel branches, keeping his eyes fixed on the girl. He did not see the colour of her eyes, only a large empty hole filled with moonlight. She let the coat fall to her feet. She unbuttoned her blouse, and took it off . . . He tripped over a soft, heavy mass on the ground, and realised to his amazement that it was a body. The beads, the robe . . . the long hair. He was suddenly afraid again. The girl was now ten metres away from him. With the cold wind from the Lure mountains blowing about her, she let slip her skirt. Underneath she was almost naked. Only two metres more to go. He reached out his hands towards the middle of her legs, wanting to feel her, run his hands over her and subdue her before killing her.

Then, before he had time to close his arms around the willing body, as he thought, with all her strength she punched her fist armed with the bunch of keys into his groin. She felt a great mass of flesh, both hard and soft, crushing under the impact. She immediately hit him again in the same place at close range, this time with the ends of the keys pointing outwards. His excitement ended suddenly with a cry overtaken by a dull gurgle. He doubled over, breathing hard like a bull bristling with banderillas. His woodcutter's hands stretched out this time to break the woman's neck, but she was no longer there. She was further away, almost invisible in the deep shadows of a holly-oak except for the curve of her belly and thighs in the moonlight. Off balance, with a pain that made it hard to breathe, the man kept on coming with outstretched arms like a gorilla. The girl fled through the trees. He followed her. He ran faster, but the distance between them did not seem to lessen. Running barefoot over the dead leaves, she tried to wear him out and, as he had been hit, he had trouble recovering. He lost sight of her. He continued searching through the laurels, cautiously, grimly. The hat under the veil fitted so firmly on his head that it had hardly moved.

Suddenly he sensed her light presence behind him. His wrist was seized in the vice-like grip of two iron hands. She pulled with all her might. It was the first time since she began judo that she had had to pull on such a formidable weight. But she had learned the technique. The man had to pick himself up from the middle of a wild rose bush.

His illusions about her had still not vanished, but his lower belly hurt him more and more, and he was holding his left wrist as he tried to flex the bruised joints in his hand.

The woman made a dash to the Mercedes. She pulled open the door as he lurched faster and faster towards her, as if he were either charging her or about to collapse. She grabbed a tiny gun from the glove box, pointed it at the man and undid the safety catch. He stopped short.

They were face to face, staring at each other. She was in full light, triumphant, almost naked, her nipples rising as she panted with excitement and fear. He was slightly bent over, recovering quickly but still anonymous, hidden behind his black veil.

They were both breathing hard. You could easily have thought that they were exhausted not by fighting but by amorous exertion.

The silence around them was profound. Even the wind had stopped blowing. All that remained in the clear night air was their breathing as they faced one another.

With the barrel of the gun at the end of her distended arm, she kept indicating Jeremy's body, and with the index finger of her left hand she pointed to the gate that the man had closed behind him. He took a long time to start doing what she wanted. She crouched back in her seat to keep out of his range but not far enough for any of the six bullets in the magazine to go wide of its mark, if need be.

It took him some time to understand what she meant, but in the end, by staring into her brightly lit face with its eyes that never wavered for a second, he knew in a few minutes what that girl was like more thoroughly than anyone would ever know her. He was no match for her.

He then made a final effort. Hauling Jeremy's body on to his shoulders, he opened the gate once again while she retrieved her various items of clothing. She dressed again, tied the belt of her coat, and followed the man past the gate to keep an eye on him and make sure that he did not take her by surprise.

The barking of foxes that were either hungry or hunted could be heard in the distance. She thought they could soon get rid of the odd bits of debris and traces of blood. The man gently laid Jeremy's body on the ground. He lifted the young man's beard and stroked the young, smooth neck.

"What a pity . . ." he murmured.

V

ALYRE MORELON HAD STAYED AWAY FROM HOME LONGER
than usual that evening to deliver a basket of truffles to the Levinkoffs.
The painter had taken up residence in an old sawmill on the Simiane
road, a kilometre past Alyre's truffle trees. He enjoyed the good opinion
of the critics and sold his paintings in America. When Alyre arrived in
the yard in front of the studio as the light was fading, he had the impression that a horde of barbarians had wiped out the whole family. A
hundred-year-old oak had been split vertically down the middle,
branches and leaves included. On the cut surface, which was as smooth
as a plank, the artist had painted trails of bluish veins in spirals and
scrolls. In the branches, scarecrows made of mauve and yellow rags
tangled and twisted on the end of coloured strings. Their poppy-red
taffeta tongues hung down at different lengths, sometimes right to the
ground, but all of them were huge and slightly phallic. The whole of
this frightening construction swayed in the evening wind.

"Well, I'll be damned!" Alyre exclaimed in admiration.

He carefully tied Roseline up to the base of the oak tree. She was
not happy.

A group of squealing kids appeared and began scurrying around
Alyre, trying to pinch truffles from the basket; scrawny dogs barked

at his heels; cats feverish with hunger fled as he approached. Then Levinkoff called out to him. He had a bass voice in a body like Job on his dunghill. He always wore shorts, and muscles like slack violin strings loosely criss-crossed his calves. Would he be sixty? Seventy? It was impossible to tell.

"What do you think of my Christmas tree?" he asked immediately.

"It's beautiful!" Alyre said.

Levinkoff ushered him towards the house. His partner was waiting on the threshold. She was the reason why Alyre was always happy to come and deliver the truffles. She was standing at the top of the four steps leading to the entrance – her favourite spot to receive visitors. Most of the time she appeared there gloriously pregnant, completely naked under a flimsy dress, her navel protruding like a lewd corkscrew. Her breasts sagged a little, but they were enormous. She was six feet tall at a guess. After he had seen her, Alyre fantasised for hours that he was drowning in her and that his hands couldn't get enough of her ample flesh. Levinkoff obviously counted on her to get a discount on the truffles. But the immovable Francine had said "300 francs a kilo", and 300 francs it would be.

They all gathered excitedly around the basket, almost dragging Alyre into the house. They sat him down and gave him a pastis, which he loathed. He managed to protect the fruits of his labours until Levinkoff had signed the cheque and it was safely in Alyre's pocket. Whereupon the kids (Levinkoff's seven children plus a little Laotian he had taken in), the pregnant goddess and the painter attacked the truffles as if they were a basket of cherries. The black juice ran out of the corners of their mouths; their strong teeth crunched on the odd bits of red earth that still clung to them. The goddess was sucking on one that must have weighed 80 grams. Her eyes were closed and her broad blond features melted with delight at the black ball that stretched her lips. In a quarter of an hour they ate 1200 francs worth of truffles. The kids were full and burping contentedly.

"Tell me, Alyre," Levinkoff said between two mouthfuls. "Did the gendarmes come to see you too?"

"Twice!" Alyre replied.

"Has another one disappeared?"

"Certainly has!" Alyre said.

"So, even in France you can't disappear if you want to without the gendarmes getting involved?"

"It looks like . . ." Alyre began saying, then stopped short.

"They sniffed around my Christmas tree for more than a quarter of an hour," Levinkoff said. "They wanted to believe that I had hung real men in my oak tree!"

"It's getting late," Alyre said, "I'm off home."

Levinkoff kissed him on both cheeks. The goddess also bent over to kiss him, and for a moment he felt the weight of her generous breasts on his shoulders. The kids also smudged truffle juice all over him. They accompanied him jubilantly to Roseline who was looking on, grunting softly. Fortunately the kids were kept at a respectful distance by the sow's 180 kilos.

Alyre set out again on the road home, with Roseline frisking about on the end of her purely symbolic leash. The winter night had fallen over the oak woods. The road the man and the sow were walking along shone white in the moonlight.

As he was passing by his truffle trees, Alyre remembered that he had left his pick in the fork of a tree. He turned and started walking over the light soil. Treading the earth under his oaks always gave him the same feeling of pleasure. He loved the silence, the gentle shade. He was a man who was content with the simple things of life.

The silence . . . The silence was disturbed some distance away by an indistinct sound that Alyre couldn't identify. It was like someone sieving earth; a gentle sound of sand being spread. At the same time he saw the metal of his pick on the fork of the tree where he had left it.

"Wait here," he said.

He let go of Roseline's leash and turned away from her to reach for his pick. Just for a second . . . Roseline, who had been anxiously sniffing the air since they heard the slight sound, moved away a little out of Alyre's range and lowered her head to the ground.

Suddenly she broke into a trot that became faster and faster. She let out a wild scream.

"Roseline!" Alyre cried.

It was too late. Roseline had escaped, dashing off into the trees. Alyre rushed after her, already panicking, his heart pounding. He found himself confronted with a hedge that the sow had easily barged through. It took him an age to get around it and climb the slope. He was frantic. He could hear his pig squealing as hard as she could through the whole of the Banon truffle woods. What had got into her head this time? Was it the call of a wild boar? It happens with sows sometimes. But it wasn't the right season for that. And anyway, that sound . . . no, it wasn't a wild boar.

He called Roseline in every direction under the clear night sky. He was filled with an awful foreboding. Suddenly he heard her scream. He dashed forward with his arms open wide, not knowing where he was going. At last he caught sight of her. She was moaning gently under a truffle oak as she tried to lick her shoulder.

"Roseline! My Roseline!"

He knelt down beside her.

"She's hurt! You're hurt, Roseline! My poor Roseline. But tell me, why are you being so stupid? Why are you so curious?"

It was hard to see as the only light came from the moon, which was screened by the branches. He felt Roseline all over. She gave a squeal of pain.

"Is that where it is, my Roseline? Is that where it hurts?"

Yes, that's where it was: a large bruise under a graze on her left shoulder and some drops of blood on the tip of one ear. Someone must have thrown stones at her. Would anyone have attacked her? Or did she try to charge a mysterious enemy who had fought back? But if that was the case, why didn't he show himself? Why did he run away? Was he a truffle thief?

"Who's the bastard . . . ?"

He looked about him furiously. If Roseline's attacker was still anywhere about, he'd better hide, thin as Alyre was! He felt he was the one who was suffering the pain in his dear Roseline's shoulder.

He quickly got his bearings. He was on the edge of several groves of oaks separated by mounds and hedges. The wind had suddenly risen with no warning, not a sound in the distance to signal its approach. Beneath the surge of air blowing down from the heights of Montsalier, Alyre heard another strange sound under the oaks. It was like the clinking of a little bell and the very soft rustling of dress material, as if the skirt of a woman in light clothes was brushing against the blackthorns by the road. Then he saw coming towards him, buffetted along the open slope between the truffle oaks by the north wind, two very different objects which were making the noise that puzzled him.

The first was a yellow plastic bucket that made a ringing sound each time it rolled over and the metal handle struck the stones. It came down a little further towards Alyre, then stuck in the low fork of a truffle oak. The other lightly bouncing object seemed to be moving on a cushion of air. Alyre knew what it was well before he could see it in detail. He knew what it was from the cold shiver that spread across his forehead.

"The *Uillaoude!*"* he whispered.

One day when he was five years old, hiding behind his grandmother who had brought him with her because he was too young to under-stand, he had seen that object with its curious bow of eight intricate loops on the head of an old woman. It hid her face completely. It was that special *mourrail*, "the incantation veil", a net endowed with magic properties by certain practices, which was meant to protect "the spell-caster" as she took part in certain particularly dangerous sessions.

It was actually nothing more than a big-brimmed hat with a *mour-rail*, a veil used by beekeepers to protect them from stings when they harvest the honey. But it was black and everything was there. It was black, battered and had belonged to a widow in the olden days. And it was also sinister because it became an incantation veil only if the widow had given fate a helping hand. If she had hastened her spouse's death by some contrivance, then bees would attack her face and could some-times kill her on the spot without the net.

* Provençal for "the lightning woman", and in this context, a woman reputed to cast spells.

Alyre took care not to touch the object, which he recognised from its large intricate bow and the black straw of the boater hat. Of course he didn't believe all those old wives' tales, but there was no harm in being on the safe side. And the things that had happened that night were very strange . . . He just watched it fluttering in the wind at his feet, and when a gust threatened to push the *mourrail* on to his shoes, he leapt back smartly.

On the other hand, the very ordinariness of the bucket was more reassuring, and Alyre had no hesitation in catching hold of it. He positioned himself so that the moonlight shone on the bottom of the bucket. It contained no more than two or three thimbles full of a granular substance that Alyre collected and weighed in his palm. It was heavy, sandy and slightly viscous. When he took it between his thumb and forefinger it stuck together like bread crumbs; it grew warm. Alyre had the impression that it was taking on a strange life of its own. He hastily got rid of it, threw the bucket away and took a long time wiping his hands down his trousers. He smelt them and made a face. He felt a queasiness he couldn't explain.

"Let's get out of here, Roseline!" he whispered.

But she was limping and it took them some time to get back to Banon. He didn't stop scolding her the whole way, he was so worried about her.

"You silly thing! What were you doing in truffle woods that don't belong to us? If Pascalon Bayle or Polycarpe Bleu or Sidoine Pipeau and Albert Pipeau the flute player had come across me – and with you into the bargain! – around their truffle trees at nine o'clock at night, we'd have been in a fine mess! And, they're all the *Uillaoude*'s nephews!

"Hang on! That's true! They're all the *Uillaoude*'s nephews. What's more, the present *Uillaoude* is the niece of the one my grandmother took me to see – and just like her . . ."

Alyre Morelon looked at the sky where the moonlight made the stars look dim. He didn't often look at the sky, but that evening he was particularly disorientated.

"Anyway Roseline, that doesn't matter . . . Strange things are happening. What was that fellow doing skulking around oak trees belonging to who knows who? With a bucket of who knows what . . . and wearing an 'incantation veil'? What use could it possibly be to him? And why wouldn't he show himself? And why did he throw stones at you?"

So many questions for just one man and a lame pig.

Once he had reached home, dragging Roseline with her head drooping under her pink ribbon, he hurried off to fetch some brandy and penicillin. He cleaned the wound in spite of her earsplitting squeals, and put a bandage on it though under no illusion that she'd keep it on for long.

"There you are. And if it's not better tomorrow, we'll take you to Dr Arnaud in Manosque."

As soon as that was done, he went to his tool shed and brought back a big padlock and screws to fix it in place. He checked the latch on the sty and pushed the padlock closed. He was just finishing when Francine arrived back and slammed her car door shut.

"For heaven's sake! What are you doing? Why on earth are you locking Roseline in? Do you think someone is likely to steal her? She squeals so much whenever a stranger comes near that I'd be surprised if . . ."

Alyre interrupted her.

"I don't think that someone might steal her," he said, "I'm afraid that someone might kill her. It's not the same thing . . ."

He went peering into the dark corners of the outhouses, as if he sensed the presence of a killer.

VI

WHEN LAVIOLETTE, STILL DRIVING HIS APPLE-GREEN VEDETTE, arrived in Banon late in the afternoon, the mistral was blowing and the square was deserted. A tiny dachshund was wandering about, obviously frightened by the wind.

Laviolette sized up the village in three glances. The first took in the cypress in the corner of a terraced garden, the last of the 150 that the monks had planted in the eighteenth century to occupy the time between prayers and to ornament the embankments. The second registered the three odd buildings with small round windows, which looked so out of place that one wondered whether they had grown out of the ground or had simply been dropped there.

They were set off by two modern hotels, one calling itself the Hôtel des Fraches and the other the Hôtel de Lure. Following their example, a development of Marseillais houses stretched out towards the high plain, each exhibiting the wealth of its imagination and its concept of art for the envy of those who passed by. Laviolette knew immediately that this Banon held no mysteries and did not concern him.

His third look, however, revealed another Banon altogether – in the person of an old man in a Basque beret who was crossing over towards the fountain, his feet at right angles as a bulwark against the mistral. Laviolette approached him and raised his hat.

"You wouldn't know a place," he asked, "where I could get fairly cheap room and board, would you?"

He purposely did not use the word "hotel".

"Room and board?" the man repeated after him.

Laviolette's hesitation allowed the old man to get a good look at the person standing opposite him. He was ordinary, neither fat nor thin, but had a large head and prominent eyes with a faraway look. He was carrying a blue sailor's kit bag that he must have brought back long ago from England slung over his shoulder. That was probably all the luggage he had.

"It might be worth taking a look," the old man said, "up at Rosemonde Burle's."

He turned towards the high part of Banon, and waving his cane indicated some cheap hostelry and the way to get there. But as he shouted through his toothless gums, the force of the mistral swept away the words as soon as they reached his lips.

"Who did you say?" Laviolette asked.

"Rosemonde Burle! At the top of the street, under the gate. It's called La Rabassière.* But I warn you! Don't tell her that I sent you. She will if she wants to . . . But if she knows it's me . . . That'll be the end of it!"

Laviolette thanked him and walked on past the café terrace, where four idlers turning up their collars behind the glass couldn't take their eyes off him. They would have given all their winnings from the Sunday horse race to know what the devil that stranger had asked Gabriel Montagnier. So much so that Laviolette has hardly gone around the corner of the square before one of them slipped outside and whipped over to the urinal where the shuffling old man had just disappeared.

The street facing Laviolette rose up steeply. Now that was the real Banon! The ground floors boasted a few little shops or a pensioner's

* The Truffle Wood.

pretty cottage with green-painted letterboxes, but you just had to look up to see three stories of ageless stone and shutters that were originally bright blue but now faded by a century of sunlight.

The road narrowed at the top of the village. Beneath the cracking layer of tar under which modern town planning had imprisoned them, you could still see the original paving stones worn smooth with use. It was there, three steps up from the street, that Laviolette found La Rabassière.

Although it was smudged, faded and cracked, the sign above the door could still be seen, pastel blue on a blistered dark background. It announced simply that here was a hotel with restaurant.

The uprights of the three window frames were carefully polished and the panes had whitening half-way up so that no-one could see in from the outside or look into the street from the inside. Laviolette pressed the latch and put his head around the door. A strong smell of truffles hit his nostrils. The room was empty. A woman's firm voice called, "I'm coming!" from the first floor.

The cellar-like room contained sixteen tables. There was a double arch near the entrance, with an invisible join, like the crossing in a church. Laviolette could not take his eyes off it, trying to work out the secret of that double vault with no visible support.

"You're looking at my ceiling? It's beautiful, eh? When I think that some mason wanted to put roughcast over it."

"A lucky escape!" Laviolette said.

He could not get over those stones, put together without cement and holding up there on their own, all due purely to the stonemason's skill.

He looked down again. Rosemonde was walking behind her counter. Her hips moved smoothly from left to right, right to left, with every step. Her figure was plump but supple.

She turned towards him.

"What is it you want?"

She was a woman of about forty, with red hair and green eyes. Her hair and breasts were luxuriant, but her mouth was thin, an indication of caution.

"It's not so much what I want, but what you can give me."

"Have you eaten?"

"Yes, thank you. No, I'm looking for somewhere to stay, where I can get room and board for about a fortnight, perhaps more . . ."

She was wiping her hands on her blouse.

"Good Lord!" she said. "With the wind that's blowing on the balcony, I got tangled up in the sheets that I was putting on the line, and I'm all wet! Wait a minute while I go and change . . . I'd be in a real fix if I caught pneumonia! Do you have a moment?"

"Yes, by all means," Laviolette said.

Her chest thrust out so firmly that it seemed unlikely to him that it could ever catch pneumonia. "She's going to think it over," he thought, "weigh up the pros and cons . . ."

She came back after three minutes.

"So, am I right in thinking that you'd like to stay here?"

"If I can."

"Well, you know . . . There's no heating. Just the flue from the stove that goes through the only room I can offer you. You see, I usually rent rooms just in the summer."

"And your room? Is that heated?"

"No! I put a river stone that's been heating all day in the oven into a stocking and take that up with me."

"A stone in a stocking! Just like my grandmother . . ." Laviolette thought.

"Well then, you'll surely have one for me?"

"Good Lord! I must have about four or five of them. There's no lack of those. Oh! Of course there's a good eiderdown . . ."

"An eiderdown as thick as this?" Laviolette asked hopefully.

"Yes!"

"And bright yellow?"

"Right again!"

"Then let me stay . . . please!"

She laughed.

"Really! That's fine . . . I'll take you! Bring your things up. It's on the first landing, opposite the stairs. But you know, you might be better off at the Hôtel de Lure!"

"Oh, no thank you!" Laviolette said. "You've seen enough of me to know that's definitely not what I want!"

VII

"WHICH ONE OF THEM IS IT?" WONDERED ALYRE.

He had just pushed open the door at Rosemonde Burle's. They were already busily engaged in the game when he entered. The baker and the priest in civvies were also there having a drink before going to knead the dough, which they did together, one helping the other. Martel the developer and Martin the plumber were discussing the schedule for a future construction site.

But the inner circle of La Rabassière patrons, those he played with, were out of the way where the light was low, quietly engaged in their game. Rosemonde was standing with her elbow on the counter, one hand on the other, looking at them calmly with a certain nostalgia.

"Which one is it?" Alyre wondered once again.

He went over to them without speaking. They didn't see him approach. He looked at them in profile, "the daggers drawn club", as they were known. They were the last truffle producers in the canton. When they died, their children would be gone or about to go, and there would be no-one left to harvest the truffles. Brushwood, bushes and weeds would cover the truffle wood for ever more, like forest submerging lost civilisations.

"I'm lucky that my Paul has definitely decided to come back here to stay, in spite of having studied at the National Agricultural Institute," Alyre thought. He couldn't help feeling some sympathy for his companions who did not have that assurance.

"And yet," he said to himself, "one of them's a bastard!"

He was thinking of Roseline's swollen leg, which was taking its time to heal, turning all the colours of the rainbow from the stones that had been thrown at her.

"I should have been watching," he said to himself, "he'd have to come to look for his *mourrail* and his bucket . . ."

He went and sat astride a chair a little further away so that he could observe them at his leisure.

They were all roughly his age, except Albert Pipeau the flute player, whose mother had been "caught" around forty, when she thought that any risk of pregnancy had passed. "Which doesn't prevent him from being handsome as a film star," she declared. But the others – Polycarpe Bleu and his brother Omer, Pascalon Bayle and his brother Virgile, Sidoine Pipeau, fifteen years older than Albert – all of those who stayed in Banon to eke out a living against the odds from a flock, a few truffle trees and 100 or so hives, had been at school with him. There were not many left. They'd either gone away, changed jobs or were already dead.

"I can't believe that one of them would have thrown stones at my sow!" Alyre thought. "They all know how valuable she is! I even lend her to them sometimes, when they haven't got a dog . . ."

He did have to admit to himself, however, that this was a rare event and never a spontaneous gesture.

The most striking thing about these men from another age, lost in this century, was the severity of their features.

"We knew that there wasn't anything to laugh about," Alyre thought. "There are problems all around us here: one year honey is scarce, the next there's a glut, but it's almost black because the bees have gathered too much pollen from the oak trees. Then the people from Marseilles don't want it. We know that lavender essence can only be sold one year in five and that you have to be patient . . . We know that there are

payments due to the Crédit Agricole bank . . . but still . . . it's no reason
for that mean, pinch-penny expression . . . Look at them! They're all
the same! Not only do they wear the same clothes – Electricity Board
linesmen's blue overalls and black oilskin cap, – but they're all so thin!
As if they won't allow themselves to put on weight in case someone
might demand something more from them! It's ruined their lives!"
Alyre concluded somewhat superficially. "And mine is happy, despite
my Francine."

Having come to this conclusion, he felt justified in taking his tobacco
pouch and his Riz-la-Croix rice papers from his pocket, and philo-
sophically rolling himself a cigarette. It was then, as he was carrying
out the precise movements involved, that he noticed someone in the
dim light on the other side of the players, sitting astride a chair as he
himself was and rolling a cigarette as though he was imitating him.
The man with the hooded eyes said nothing, but was observing the
other profile of the card players with great attention, just as Alyre was
doing from his side.

Everyone knew by now that he was someone in the police force, and
that he was investigating the recent disappearances, ostensibly "in the
family's interest". "How could tramps like them have a family," Alyre
wondered, "and one that still took an interest in them? Since he's so
interested in the families of hippies, why couldn't he also be interested
in my sow? I've had the feeling for a while now that my Roseline's in
danger . . ."

He shivered. He had visions of that plump, pink neck . . . so vulner-
able . . . so coveted by butchers . . .

He shook himself. "You're absolutely crazy . . . Who would want to
kill your pig? And why?"

His musing was interrupted by one of the players losing his temper
with another, who had done something stupid. It was Polycarpe Bleu,
quivering with the violent tic that came over him at times, berating
his partner Sidoine Pipeau, the wood merchant. The other pair,
Pascalon Bayle and Omer Bleu, had gathered up the cards and were
waiting for the row to end with that noncommittal look of people

who are very glad that they are not the ones making a spectacle of themselves.

"Just look how happy they are to see their brothers involved in a slanging match!" Alyre said to himself. "Their brothers are not close to their hearts, that's for sure! I've often wondered why they all insist on coming to play in the same bar, since they haven't been on speaking terms for twenty years! It must be for convenience . . . or else it's for Rosemonde . . . Of course she's not Levinkoff's wife, but still . . ."

The other Pipeau brother Albert, who was also watching the game, from the side of the table, bought into the argument purely to aggravate the situation. An explosion of hatred, quite out of proportion to a difference of opinion about the play, suddenly erupted among these inscrutable men who had known each other all their lives. They secretly harboured good reasons for not liking each other but also for staying together as much as possible. That way they could keep an eye on each other and always know what was going on.

"Good reasons," Alyre thought. "What better reason that disappointment in love? Mind you, it was sheer stupidity that caused the quarrel between Polycarpe and Omer. That's hardly surprising given their long sanctimonious faces . . . And yet they shared the same bathtub as boys, so to speak. When they were little, they were always covered in blotches during the summer because they were washed so often. My mother wouldn't let me play with them . . . Their self-esteem has certainly risen since then. One has had a career in the army, with years on double pay . . . Now he's retired at forty-four with his 200 hectares, which he rents out in winter to the shepherd in Larche, thank you very much! His brother Omer has always remained here with a woman from Saint-André, who brought a bit of money with her. He even had vines – all Jacquez grapes. One day Polycarpe, who has always been the oracle of the family, said to him, and it was well-intentioned, 'You should dig up your vines!'—'What do you mean, dig them up? They're the only thing that'll grow around here!'— 'You know they're Jacquez and Jacquez are prohibited, and most important of all, they cause cancer?'—'You'd be the only cancer around here, wouldn't you?' Well, one thing led to another . . . Polycarpe wrote an anonymous letter denouncing him to the Taxation Department supposedly to save his life! Omer went out looking for him with a shotgun full of buckshot. Everyone got involved: the gendarmes, the priest, the mayor. They managed to get them to shake hands in front of everybody. The brothers withdrew their hands as if they were on fire. Their mother on her deathbed begged them to kiss and make up. They did. I was there, and they were puffing and blowing like a couple of warring wild boars. They've got used to the situation since then, but not a word have they spoken to each other. They play cards. But never together. They play boules, but never utter a word!"

The dispute was calming down. There were still mutterings between the disgruntled partners, but they began playing again. You could hear Pascalon Bayle licking his thumb with each card dealt. The stranger astride his chair was now watching Alyre, who looked uneasy as though he had something to hide. He walked round the table and put a friendly hand on Alyre's shoulder.

"And what about you?" he asked. "You're not playing?"

"Oh, I'm just watching," Alyre said.

"You have the farm near Montsalier, as you leave Banon, don't you?"

"Right!" Alyre said.

The stranger nodded, walked round the table again and went back to his chair.

"He won't get far asking questions like that . . ." Alyre thought.

But from where he was sitting, he noticed shoulders hunching slightly as the man walked behind the players and observers of the game. Even Pascalon Bayle, who was about to throw down a card, gave a sidelong glance, as if he suspected some kind of nasty trick.

"They're slippery characters," Laviolette thought. "You'd swear they'd eliminated anything that would let you get to grips with them."

"Which of those bastards was in the truffle woods last night and nearly killed Roseline?"

He peered as close up as he could get at his two childhood friends, Pascalon and Virgile Bayle. Those two had also quarrelled. They were what you might call unusual characters. Alyre remembered that during the war Virgile, who was seventeen at the time, had once stayed calmly leaning on his elbow in the sun for three hours while the Germans patrolled the entire hill looking for two Resistance fighters. Virgile had got them to lie on their stomachs in the middle of a still flock of sheep that he kept in order just by whistling! His brother Pascalon is a pilferer. He has hardly any land with truffle trees but he always sells more truffles than us, and we have a lot . . . There's something wrong there! . . . He rules the family at home. His two daughters clean his shoes for him. He put his mother into an old people's home. He does agricultural valuations, and if you want a good one, you have to grease his palm. Well, those two also quarrelled, but in their case, even I can't remember why. They live in a pair of semi-detached houses with wives who talk to each other quite happily. But not those two. No-one knows why. One day we thought we'd found the reason. They were shouting at each other over the garden wall, with about twenty metres between them. But it wasn't possible to come closer for fear of being seen, and the mistral was blowing a gale! Couldn't hear a thing. Nothing! Since then no-one has heard either of them. Not only do they refuse to speak to each other, but they can scarcely bring themselves to reply to anyone else.

What are the thoughts that have been knocking around for years in the heads under those caps – thoughts that will never come out, never be articulated? No-one, not even God the Father, could make these die-hards give in. They knew what they knew, and that was that . . . Every man for himself. No pity. Uncivilised types feel comfortable living that way . . .

Alyre pushed his chair back a bit so that he could also see the two nephews of the *Uillaoude*: Sidoine and Albert Pipeau. Sidoine is well-off. He sold half the Lure harvest to Italian management for twenty years. At one time, he employed fifteen Portuguese between Lardiers and Saint-Étienne. He doesn't want to do it any more. He claims the labour costs are too high . . . He's a handsome man, but his brother Albert . . . Just take a look at him!" Alyre thought resentfully. "Incidentally, he's called 'the flute player' because he walks faster than anyone else."

This same Albert with his superior smile was leaning back in his chair, legs outstretched, hands in pockets, crotch bulging in his tight trousers. He had a straight nose and low forehead, with short dark curls drooping over his prominently curved eyebrows. It was hard to tell the colour of his eyes.

"See how happy he is! But it's for the wrong reasons. Will you look at that! Even Rosemonde is playing up to him! She gives him a good eyeful of her breasts when she bends over to serve his drink. I wouldn't be surprised if Francine . . ."

He was now staring so intently that Albert felt it, despite his vain self-satisfaction, and turned his head. Alyre lowered his eyes to hide his intense dislike of the man.

"I'm certainly not the most unfortunate one," he thought. "That brother of his! He's a good enough reason to be on bad terms for fifteen years! And it's a reason you certainly don't come across every day!"

He was really tempted to open his mouth and call out to them merrily, "Do you remember, both of you?" He restrained himself with some difficulty, but couldn't resist the pleasure of looking at Sidoine with a certain amount of commiseration as he remembered the story.

He had just married a girl called Victoire whom he met up north in the Drôme. Albert had just finished his military service. She hadn't seen him yet! Late one winter evening she was hurrying round the corner of the church to Gardon's to buy some sugar. (She's told the story a hundred times since, to the whole of Banon . . .) Right on the corner – talk about fate at work! – she bumps into him, and in the time it takes to realise what's happening, he's opened his arms and she hasn't had time to say a thing! What chance did she have to resist a man like a marble statue? After all, she came from Dieulefit. She'd never seen anyone like him! Afterwards . . . It lasted a week. She couldn't hold out any longer. "That's love," she kept repeating, "yes, that's it, that's love!" When she found out that he was Sidoine's brother, she told her husband everything. They're not all like my Francine . . . They patrolled the *Uillaoude*'s chestnut trees like enemies in wartime, taking shots at each other. The gendarmes brought them back in handcuffs and black with

43

gunpowder. It cost them a 1000-franc fine and six months suspended sentence. That calmed them down a bit but . . . it wouldn't do for one of them to come upon the other bending over the side of a well, I can tell you.

He sighed. "When you think of all that! Life's a strange thing, eh? Now Victoire's breasts hang down to her waist. She's had five children. She lets herself go. Love is over for her. She could run round the corner of the church a hundred times . . . It would never happen again!"

"Which one could it be?" Alyre wondered once again. "They're both the *Uillaoude*'s nephews. But she doesn't do that sort of thing now . . . She could have left her *mourrail* lying about anywhere. It doesn't matter. The other night my Roseline saw something she shouldn't. I'll have to keep an eye on her . . ."

He was the last to leave because Rosemonde had to pay him for some eggs. When he closed the door behind him, all his table companions had gone home in their cars. The only person left in the small square around the fountain was Laviolette in his overcoat, taking a piss against the wisteria on the presbytery wall while gazing at the moon.

"I say, Superintendent . . ."

Alyre began walking towards him to do likewise.

Laviolette turned round and saw the short man who seemed to know a thing or two approaching the wisteria while fiddling with his fly.

"Have you something to tell me?" he said.

"Someone has attacked my sow!" Alyre said.

He told him what had happened two nights ago. Well . . . almost everything. For although he described Roseline dashing off into the trees and her squeal of pain, although he gave a detailed account of her wound, he was careful not to say a word about the bucket and the *mourrail*. All that was too personal. He could still see the black lace at his feet rippling in the wind as if it had a life of its own. No. You don't speak to the police about these mysteries you don't believe in.

"Do you have any enemies?" Laviolette asked.

"Oh, no, of course not!"

"Deceived husbands don't have enemies," Alyre thought bitterly.

"People are always very indulgent to a deceived husband. They clap him on the shoulder. They say, 'Ah yes, Alyre!' full of bonhomie, showing what they think about his situation."

"You know," Laviolette said, "if your sow charged someone, it's not surprising that he defended himself. She could have been taken for a wild boar."

"All pink and clean as she is?"

"Well, you know, at night . . ."

Alyre shook his head. And, of course . . . That wasn't the only thing . . .

"By the way," he exclaimed as they were doing up their flies with inordinate care, "do you think it's possible . . . do *you* think it's normal for . . . for . . . for someone to mistake the squeal of a sow for a wild boar?"

"Why not?" Laviolette replied.

But he had the impression that the little man had changed his mind, and that he really wanted to ask him something entirely different.

VIII

"MY PRESENCE HERE IS NOT EXACTLY OFFICIAL NOR EXACTLY regular," Laviolette said. "In fact, I'm tiptoeing around this investigation . . ."

"*They*'ve told me about your mission," replied Viaud, the senior officer of the gendarmerie. "*They*'ve asked me to give you all possible assistance . . ."

"And manpower if need be, I know," Laviolette sighed. "I'll have no lack of help. I can also call on Marseilles."

"An investigation on behalf of the families concerned won't need that, surely?" Viaud said.

"Probably not. It's not a black-and-white investigation. It has to be done unobtrusively . . . Besides, *they* made no bones about it when they phoned me. 'As you're unremarkable,' I was told, 'you blend in anywhere, you're not much to look at . . .' I'm summarising, of course . . . They didn't say it to me all at once . . . But," he added, this time turning to the sergeant, "do you really think I look as ordinary as all that?"

The two gendarmes burst out laughing.

Viaud got up and took a beige file containing copies of various case reports from his cupboard.

"It hadn't escaped my notice, you know," he said, "that all these disappearances stand out in comparison with other similar cases . . ."

"How?" Laviolette asked.

"The fact that the trail stops at Banon, a village of 900 inhabitants. Before coming here I was stationed in Remiremont, an industrial town of 40,000 inhabitants. In goods years or bad, we had ten to fifteen disappearances to deal with, nearly always girls who nearly always turned up on the Côte d'Azur . . . or in Irun . . . So, six in Banon! In six months!"

"And who don't turn up on any Côte d'Azur!" Laviolette pointed out.

"Here are the reports on each case plus interviews with the people looking for them."

In most cases it was a letter from the father or mother noted by the police station nearest to them. Only one undertook the trip to Banon. All of them had supplied details that indicated nicely brought-up children: blazers, school ties, Bally shoes; and for the girls: jeans, jumpers, birthday trinkets. At the time of the last meeting with their parents, all of them were wearing wristwatches given by their families, and all were clean and smooth-faced. The photos showed typical middle-class teenagers. Even Constantin Spirageorgevich – a name to conjure with – was not a foreigner at all, but the son of a Parisian accountant. Even Ismaël Ben Amozil was the offspring of an honest Le Sentier wholesaler who sold t-shirts by the cubic metre and piles of djellabas from his warehouse.

"But was the son actually a plumber?"

"Indeed he was. It was his first act of defiance against his father. At sixteen he became an apprentice to a heating engineer in the Rue Oberkampf."

"Jeremy Piochet . . ."

"I've heard that name somewhere," Laviolette said.

"Of course you have. If you have a good plastic bucket or basin at home, you'll have seen his name embossed on the bottom."

"Oh, so that's it!"

"Yes. His mother has just died. He and his sister own a big business at La Cluse, near Oyonnax."

Viaud stopped for a moment, with a dreamy look in his eye.

"She's gorgeous . . ." he added.

"Who is?"

"His sister."

"You know her?"

"She's here in Banon . . . waiting . . . wandering about. She's inconsolable. If you saw her . . . With her fair complexion and blonde hair . . . She looks like an angel!"

"Come now, Chief . . ." Laviolette said.

"I promised to find her brother for her!"

"Dead or alive?"

"I didn't specify."

Laviolette sighed.

"That leaves the girls who were last heard of on that date," he said.

"Incarnacion Chinchilla . . . Niece of the man who owns the Les Lusiades hotel in Irun. He came here too, but left again. He adores his niece. He kept kissing the photo of her that he had brought with him. In the end I began to wonder if . . ."

"Yes. You wondered whether he wasn't a bit fixated on her . . . So that the niece would have had every reason in the world to take to the road."

"Very likely. Strange as it may seem, Patricia McKetterick was probably in a similar situation. In her case, it was her stepfather. She inherited a distillery in Dundee, in Scotland."

"A distillery? In Scotland?"

"Yes, whisky. But the brand isn't known outside Britain. It's kept for home consumption. We have a few more details about this Patricia McKetterick. With the neck of a beer bottle that she'd just broken, she lacerated the jowls of a fifty-year-old who was brushing his hand over her behind. It happened at Le Perpendiculaire, Rue Saint-Benoît in Paris. She was drunk, and it seems she shouted, 'You're as disgusting as my stepfather!' It's there in the dossier . . . a report from the police station of the 6th *arrondissement*."

"A real psychodrama . . ." Laviolette murmured. "And both are girls prone to them . . . Rather than teach others a lesson, it's more likely they needed treatment themselves, don't you think?"

"Probably," Viaud replied.

Laviolette examined the five enlarged photos spread out in front of him. Five young faces as different from each other as they could be. Their eyes, however, had the same look, which was no help as it belonged to a whole section of the younger generation. It clearly meant: "It's no use talking to them; it's no use explaining to them. They wouldn't understand! They're too bloody stupid!"

Laviolette sighed. What had become of them with their undirected spirit of rebellion – a result of their minds being warped by their elders' deplorable lack of answers to their sense of alienation? How did their faces look now? What had become of their bodies? Were they dead or alive? And why Banon?

"You understand, Superintendent," Viaud said, "that these photos show them *before*. Months have passed between when they were taken and the time the person ends up in Banon. Months of hitchhiking, walking through the countryside, nights under little bridges. Not washing, not shaving. Along the way they've put some sort of stuff into their hair and they're all a mahogany colour. They've smoked pot and the expression in their eyes has changed dramatically. By the time they arrive here, they all look the same: as if they had been lying for a month in a muddy pond before being fished out. That's how they look as they pass by . . . So you can show your photos all you like! No-one has ever seen them as they used to look. We've shown these documents to some-thing like 300 people. No-one has recognised a single one . . . hasn't even hesitated with their answer!"

"Even the ones up there in Montsalier . . ."

"That's our regular beat. We often go in the van, sometimes on foot, and when we get up there through the Le Deffens woods . . ."

"So you didn't learn anything up there either?"

Viaud began to laugh. "Learn anything! It's easy to see that you don't mix with types like these! You see them up there slumped around a fire of green wood, looking grim. You show the photos. Nothing. No response.

No-one bats an eyelid. You walk around among them and you end up feeling like a ghost. They just don't see you! And don't even think of laying a hand on one of their shoulders. They'd collapse, yelling that they've been bashed!"

"You'd think that the disappearance of several of their kind would worry them."

"Nothing worries them. They know how and why people disappear."

"Don't they have any contact with the people in the district?"

"Yes they do. They're taken on as casual labour in the summer to help with bringing in the hay and gathering potatoes and melons. Yes, there are contacts! You might even say that apart from the odd goat that mysteriously goes missing, the population is perfectly adapted to this kind of tourism."

As they were talking, Laviolette had straddled a chair and was carefully rolling a cigarette.

"And what's your personal opinion?" he asked.

"In all probability they're somewhere else . . . Kathmandu, Benares, Punta Arenas . . . Who knows?" He got up and looked through the window at the winter landscape. "All the same . . . There's something strange about all this . . . I'm starting to wonder whether they weren't right to send you."

"And I'm starting to wonder whether you couldn't deal with it . . . ?"

"Yes . . . oh! Mind you . . . Well, actually," he said, suddenly making up his mind, "as far as the girls are concerned, there *is* one strange detail. We made inquiries at the Post Office and were told by the postmaster that on 18 October two young women by the name of Patricia McKetterick and Incarnacion Chinchilla were each sent a money order by telegraph from two Parisian stockbrokers. Two days earlier two girls had sent telegrams singing themselves Patricia and Incarnacion. Now those money orders were never picked up."

"Were they large sums?"

"2500 and 3000 francs. That's off the record. We can't mention it in our report. After the regulation time had elapsed, the postmaster credited these money orders to the senders' accounts."

"Everything would suggest that Patricia and Incarnacion have never left Banon."

"Indeed . . . With most people that would be obvious, but with hippies it's quite another story. You see, apart from them looking alike, the thing that makes our investigations even more difficult is the fact that they are always on the move. You think they're sleeping peacefully alone or in couples on an old mattress on the ground . . . Don't you believe it! Suddenly at about two in the morning, whatever the weather, the urge to escape takes hold of them."

"You use the word 'escape', but from what?"

"Anything . . . their fantasies, their memories. Nearly all of them have unbearable ones that go back to their childhood, and which seem to be stirred on certain nights . . . In short, when it happens, they get up and go, without a word to the person they may be sleeping with that night or to anyone else. They step over the other sleepers and, barefoot or badly shod, their guitars slung over their backs, they disappear into the night. You can follow their progress from hamlet to hamlet by the sound of the dogs barking. We stop them sometimes, but what valid reason do we have to detain them? How can we establish an itinerary of their wanderings? They always have enough money for them not be considered as vagrants. And as for their permanent address, it's their parents' in Paris! And believe me, it's more often in wealthy Ranelagh than in working-class Belleville! That's to show you that the two girls could send for money when they were hungry and then leave, whereas when they were completely stoned and incapable of remembering anything . . ."

"Yes, I see what you mean. But after that, hasn't there been any sign of them anywhere?"

"Not as far as I know."

"And you would know. It would be in this pitifully thin file. And you would also know if the three others had been questioned. So here we have five people on the missing persons' list and not one of them has been seen by police anywhere. The first dates back three months, and the most recent two weeks. If that wasn't the case, you'd know it, having instigated the search."

"No doubt."

"Of course it would be futile to draw any premature conclusions, but . . . do you believe the theory of a sudden departure?"

"Well . . . to tell the truth, not a lot. But that's more from intuition than logic. Consequently my opinion isn't worth much.

"Right! I agree with you, so that makes two worthless opinions. We'll wait for logic to come to us . . ."

He got up. The chief followed suit.

"Naturally, I haven't come here to trespass on your patch," Laviolette said. "Not only am I here on a visit, but I'm also here with no job to do and no authority to do anything . . . I'm here for almost for no reason."

"In short, you're here to immerse yourself in the atmosphere of the place."

"That's it! Yes, that's it! I'm here to immerse myself in the atmosphere of the place."

"Anyway, you can count on me. If anything comes up, I won't try to interpret it on my own . . ."

They shook hands, silently acknowledging their mutual understanding.

Outside on the esplanade going down towards the hospital, dust was swirling between the heavily pruned plane trees. Banon was riding the wind that swept all before it. Dead leaves torn from the undergrowth were whipped against the north-facing walls. The sky was black. There was no moon.

At ten o'clock the streets were deserted. All that could be heard was the occasional sound of a badly tuned television set or the flame-gun at the bakery, where the owner and the priest were heating up the oven.

Laviolette noticed that not far from his "charabanc", as he called his Vedette, another car was parked under the lopped plane trees. It was metallic blue, thick as a tank and sturdy as a van.

He also saw the dog that was there when he arrived. It limped from house to fountain; it wandered under the elms of the former hotel, which had closed down long ago, then over to the walls of the new Post Office. Sometimes it timidly tried to stand up and push against a green rubbish bin, but they were all closed. Local dogs only managed to tip them over at about five in the morning when their exasperated owners finally let them out.

"It's lost," Laviolette thought. "I'll have to do something."

The wind was whipping his uncovered face, but he dawdled along whistling a cheerful tune for as long as the cold would let him. He headed in a roundabout way towards the thin little dachshund.

"If all the things I wish on the bastard who dumped this animal come to pass, he certainly won't make old bones!" Laviolette thought.

The dachshund must have tried to avoid so many kicks over the last few days that it had become very wary. Laviolette's gentle advances drew no response. Every time he got within at least ten métres, the dog barked in panic and ran further away.

"I'll have to corner him at the garage," Laviolette said to himself out loud.

Next to the Hôtel des Fraches was a huge carriage entrance leading to an area with a mud floor for carriages and carts. It had not changed for a century. The doors were still there, but they were so heavy that people had long ago given up trying to close them. In summer the stable was used to house clients' carriages. It still harboured an old coach made by the master wheelwright Vinatier in the 1880s, eternally unharnessed and half-hidden under a wall of empty crates. You could still see the artistically painted banners on the sides announcing its route: Banon–Revest-du-Bion.

Laviolette had succeeded little by little in bringing the suspicious animal back towards the dark entrance, but as soon as he tried to shoo it in, the dachshund would jump out of the way with a plaintive bark.

"I'll never manage it alone!" Laviolette sighed, thinking aloud. "Certainly not in this wind, which must be upsetting it . . . The worst thing is I don't know its name! That's why there's nothing in the world more lost than a dog without its master. It had a name. People called it by that name. Then all of a sudden, it's left with nothing: nothing to eat, nothing to love, and no name. Can you imagine that?"

After a lot of effort, he finally managed to drive the dachshund once more into the darkness of the porch. He began the litany of lost dogs, which he knew so well, "Come here, you poor little thing! You won't be unhappy up there in the fresh air at Piégut. Old Ricandance, who is already taking care of eight of you for me, he'll look after you so well. And he'll find a name for you again. You'll be in clover!"

He tried to trap it under a vegetable crate. The dachshund was dizzy with tiredness, misery and hunger, but it feared man above all else. The dog no longer trusted anyone.

It got away from Laviolette. The superintendent tried to catch it, but it ran out of the storeroom and made off towards the Revest road, where it disappeared from sight.

"How can I make it understand," Laviolette thought, "that not all men are bastards?"

IX

"GO UP THROUGH 'THE VALLEY OF SIGHS'," ROSEMONDE TOLD him when he asked the way to Montsalier.

"The Valley of Sighs". Well, it certainly lived up to its name. Under the mass of clouds combed through leafless branches, there was nothing but dead trees killed by lightning, riddled by vermin and destroyed by hunters to put up perches for the birds they use as lures. They killed the trees by knocking carpenters' nails into the trunks. The loose stones on the steep slopes tumbled over each other in the violent wind. The tinkling bells of a flock could be heard somewhere far off in the countryside.

Laviolette got out of his car and gazed glumly at the steep path ahead. When one is "of a certain age", smokes a lot, drinks a bit and has a few minor medical problems, being faced with a suddenly rising path is anything but exciting. He started off briskly nonetheless, puffing and grumbling to himself. Buffeted by squalls of wind, sometimes advancing with his mouth open like a fish out of water, sometimes suddenly pushed back a metre by the storm and flattened against the burnt trunk of a mulberry tree that had been dead for a hundred years, he finally reached the windmills on top of the cliff. They sat at various distances from each other, but all of them had lost their top half. Nothing remained to show that they ever had sails or the heavy wooden machinery that turned the grindstones. And yet Laviolette thought he could make out the sound of a spinning wheel under the howling of the wind.

He was walking sideways like a crab. The mist flowed around him as he battled against the current like someone in danger of drowning. Sometimes the wind sent it streaming up almost to the clouds. Then he could suddenly see sixty kilometres of land softly lit by the invisible sun: right up to the Vallon des Toupins, Chastelar de Lardiers and the outskirts of the Mont Ventoux, whose head was still kept hidden from curious eyes. He noticed that the Carniol Woods and the Albion Forests were dotted with well-tended open spaces like clearings, but too tidy, too symmetrical. These seemingly harmless sights were enough to send a shiver through a sensitive soul like Laviolette.

As he gazed at them, Laviolette's thoughts were distracted by a strange humming sound, which turned out to be the hum of a prayer wheel. Firmly planted in the centre of a cairn, it buzzed as it turned around and around anti-clockwise in the wind. Laviolette stood there among the silky strands of mist, gazing at it in disbelief. Someone had actually carried this lantern pole, which now presented its revolving parchments to the biting wind of the Basses-Alpes, from somewhere in the depths of Asia. (Had it been bought, stolen, or what?)

"Someone," Laviolette thought, "who will try to hang his lantern anywhere . . . Someone driven completely crazy, lost far in the crowd, out of sight of Descartes and Montaigne . . . sandwiched between the ugliness of mankind and the beauty of the world. That's the way I see it. I understand them. They're right."

He made his way among the ruins. A few front steps had been cleared here and there. Dry nettles rattled their stalks against each other and the branches of dead fennel. A dead fig tree creaked with each gust of wind.

Laviolette located the church from the flapping of tent canvas. The vagrants had attached them as best they could to the beams that were still intact in the holes in the roof. They had added some of the thick plastic that market gardeners roll out to protect their vegetables. The whole thing was fastened down with heavy tiles and flat roofing stones from the ruins, which rattled dangerously overhead near the empty bell tower.

The Romanesque roll mouldings had been stolen long ago. A large part of the porch, which had lost its supports, had fallen on to the step to the forecourt. You had to climb over a pile of rubble to reach it.

Laviolette clambered over it and walked towards the centre of the church occupied by the font. It was a bowl full of rainwater. On the unbroken flagstones under the blind rose window that let some daylight in, there was a fitful kind of fire made of holly, smoking and sending out sparks. A few damp oak roots had been tossed on the fire, which did nothing to improve it. The smoke wafted about looking for a way out. It drifted in waves under the crumbling barrel vaults, but there was still enough at ground level to make Laviolette's eyes water.

He thought at first that the den was empty, then he noticed two big sleeping bags curled up on a sagging metal base. The zips were almost completely closed. The only thing poking out of either of the openings was the top of a mop of dirty hair. One of the bags suddenly sat upright, the zip opened and a magnificent Brahmin head with flowing beard appeared before Laviolette. He seemed about forty-five. His almond eyes were wide open, but the look he gave the superintendent was one of unconcern. He was trying to decide whether it was worthwhile coming back to the land of the living or not. He decided against it and the sleeping bag fell back on to the broken base. A long hand with tapering fingers felt around for the tab and zipped it up as far as it would go without smothering the occupant. The bag gave a few jerks, then lay still.

A brand-new individual septic tank made of plastic had been used as a table.

"Where the hell did they pinch that?"

Three half-empty litre bottles of wine had been left there on the lid beside two-thirds of a loaf of bread and a tobacco pouch. Under the low sacristy door blocked up by rubble, a goat with full udders was tethered near a heap of stripped branches.

"Those loonies wouldn't even get up to milk the goat!" Laviolette thought.

Loud grunting noises, like a woodcutter at work, were emanating from behind the altar. The apse had collapsed on to the tabernacle, which was buried under the debris. A cheap candlestick covered with dirty plaster dust was stuck in it like a holy relic. You could still see traces of candle in the blackened cup.

Laviolette walked around the obstacle. Screened by the rubble, and naked under their sleeveless sheepskin shirts, a vigorous young pair were making love, with the girl on top. The man, who had a golden beard, was lying on a thick, open sleeping bag. The girl was astride this robust blond lad, who was doing all he could to make her grunt and groan with the effort. His grubby hand lay on the faded name of some minor noble buried under the flagstone several centuries ago.

Their eyes were open and did not even blink when Laviolette suddenly appeared before them. They continued their exertions and experiments without a moment's pause.

"The gendarme was right," Laviolette thought, "to them we really are just ghosts."

The strangest thing about these drop-outs was that they ended up seeing the world they rejected as insubstantial; its crude reality faded to the same ghostly evanescence as their drug-induced dreams.

The couple, the two creatures sleeping on the mattress, and the smoke were the only occupants of the place. What had Laviolette hoped to find when he decided to make the climb? Even if he kicked their backsides, the four dreamers wouldn't be of any help.

He was about to leave when he noticed something at the end of the transept. Piled against a votive altar of some saint or other, whose image had been worn away through the years, was a cubic metre pyramid of detritus: without any doubt it was their communal rubbish heap. His eyes lit up at this windfall. Judging by the successive layers and the more or less rotten smells emanating from it, this rubbish tip had been used by the community for some time. Sprayed by the urine and vomit of those who were reluctant to go outside on certain nights, this archeological find drew Laviolette to it like a wasp to a piece of roast meat.

"Of course," he thought, "this is hardly work for a superintendent ... And of course the gendarmes could have realised before I have that this tip was a nest of clues. But to search through it with all the attention it demands, you need to have a real love for archeology." Crouching in front of this gold mine, he took a deep breath.

"And a strong stomach," he added as an afterthought.

He sorted though it with great care, carefully putting various containers of no interest to his right, and on his left, everything such as notes, pieces of paper, handbills, envelopes, to be examined later.

The light coming through the rose window was dim and he had left his glasses in the car. He treated bits of broken bottle and razor blades that could pierce his gloves very warily. However, he did keep a few hypodermic needles and broken syringes. He tipped the lot into a rusty biscuit tin. All that would be sent back to the lab. with precise specifications.

His fingers hooked long trails of used tampons and sanitary pads stuck to each other like garlands. Almost unidentifiable bits of meat, still only rotted in parts after several weeks, clung stubbornly to his gloves. There was nothing, however, to rival the bottoms of tin cans. The mixture of rusty iron and rotten fish made an olfactory cocktail that was almost unbearable.

Nonetheless, he went about the task enthusiastically and methodically, spurred on by the song of love rising and falling like a leitmotif from behind the altar, to the rhythm of the cries of surprise produced by each new convulsion.

As he went down deeper into the heart of the tip, he was overcome by a feeling that is well known to archeologists: the conviction that someone had excavated that rubbish heap before him. Dirty posters of Che Guevara, all kinds of old junk forgotten by everyone were on a level near the top while scraps of notices for recent demonstrations were right down among the coffee grounds. Potato peel and the tops of leeks were still fresh under twenty centimetres of indescribable refuse, while stuff that was mouldy and almost rotted down to humus had been brought to the surface. In short, the chronological order had been disrupted. That made him persevere despite the constant revolting smell.

The clue was sitting on the compost of rotted garbage at the bottom. It was a backpack without pockets or frame – the small version designed for solo climbers. Laviolette felt immediately and intuitively that the rubbish heap had been excavated expressly to hide that object.

"Too new, too clean, not smelly enough to have been there for as long as you would expect at the depth where I found it."

He opened it with some difficulty, as the leather straps had swollen in their metal buckles. He took out a school exercise book, a copy of the *Georgics* and an unopened tin of dog food.

"Surely they don't eat that?" he wondered.

An early twilight was filling the church. Laviolette could no longer see anything clearly. Anyway, he thought he had reached the layer of rubbish that pre-dated the first disappearance. The couple behind the altar were still making love; they had simply changed positions. The two sleeping bags were still lying there on the broken base like two huge beans. Laviolette left the church, the biscuit tin in one hand and the backpack in the other.

Outside the church, the prayer wheel was still turning at full speed. The wind was getting stronger, but it had not dispersed the mist. Laviolette went down the stony path towards the haven of his car. But he was not alone in the gale. The tinkling bells of a flock of sheep could be heard on the opposite side of the valley.

"A shepherd?" Laviolette thought. "He must often pass this way . . . I wonder if he knows anything."

He put the biscuit tin and the backpack into the boot and set off again. He made his way as best he could, trying to follow the sound of the bells. He went up a slope that was as slippery underfoot as a heap of gravel. He stopped frequently to get his bearings from the various noises borne on the wind: the familiar one of the flock in search of something; another much more indistinct, sometimes loud, sometimes so tenuous that you thought you'd imagined it . . .

A huge gust of wind whipped about him, suddenly dispersing the mist and opening a hole in the clouds right up to the blue sky. Laviolette could then make out the flock standing in a spiral, nose to tail, bleating like lost souls. Two goats were doing the same on the roof of a hovel which had once been a farm. Stretched out on a flagstone at the foot of a wall lay some sort of shepherd wrapped in an old prisoner-of-war coat, his chin resting on his hand. He had a beard, a shock of untidy hair, and wide eyes that seemed to be waiting for something extraordinary to be revealed to him. Two dogs, heads to one side, ears twitching, were just as attentive, in fact so absorbed that they did not hear the stones rolling under Laviolette's feet.

All three were pointing their noses towards a gap of fifty centimetres – hardly wide enough for a man to pass through – that split the ground on the vast, even expanse of rock. The name of this hole was written beside it in red lead paint that had slowly faded in the weather: Gouffre de Caladaïre.

A kind of whispering music made by the gale rose up from the hole, and this was what was fascinating the shepherd and the dogs.

Laviolette decided that the time had come to bring the shepherd back to earth before the young man was tempted to follow the wind and its music into the hole. It looked harmless enough, but there was a sheer drop of 400 metres into darkness.

"Hellooo," he called out. "Where you goin' down there?"

The dogs rushed towards Laviolette's feet. They were two surly-looking mongrels of unknown origin, both with wall eyes, one black, the other aquamarine blue. They stopped a metre away from Laviolette, barking furiously as if they had seen a viper.

"Trusco! Toulouse!" the shepherd shouted, although he was wasting his breath.

Laviolette advanced up the narrow space between the two sets of dog fangs, twenty centimetres from his trouser legs. The dogs gave up in any case as soon as he shook the hand of their master, who waved them off to round up the sheep.

"How are you, all right?"

"Orright." The shepherd said. "You takin' a walk?"

"You take the sheep out in weather like this?"

"You don't worry about the fog?"

"You find much for them to eat?"

"You lost yer way?"

This style of conversation, made up of a series of questions between two people determined not to reply but ask a question themselves, could have gone on for some time. However, Laviolette soon gave up this approach and went straight to the point.

"I'm looking for my daughter," he said right out of the blue. "You wouldn't have come across her by any chance?"

Only people used to going out in all conditions could explain a family walk on such a miserable day by saying that they were taking a chance on the weather. He decided against that explanation. Anyway, when the shepherd replied, it was only to Laviolette's second question.

"Oh!" he said. "I don't do it for them to find something to eat . . . They're fed inside. But the boss wants 'em to be taken out in all kinds of weather. She says that bad weather makes the lambs strong. She's some woman, the boss, I can tell yer!"

The expression on his face said it all.

"Right!" Laviolette interrupted him. "My daughter's a bit like that. You wouldn't have seen her by any chance?"

The shepherd was gazing at the horizon as if to round up a flock of smoke, whereas his own was being kept well in its place by the dogs.

"When did you lose 'er?"

"A while ago! One . . . two months . . . She was dressed up like a tramp. And she had an English accent!" he added on a sudden inspiration.

"Oh! Well," the shepherd said, "if she 'ad an English accent . . ."

His mop of hair shook vigorously from side to side to signify that there was no hope. He emphasised the point by waving his stick around in the air several times, indicating the vastness of the world, the uncertainty of things, the futility of looking for a needle in a haystack.

"Those girls," he said at last, "they all look the same, yer know!"

"Don't I know it!" Laviolette replied, despondently.

"But . . ." the shepherd continued, drawing closer to the superintendent, "if she 'ad an English accent . . . A month ago, maybe two, let's say five weeks . . . There could 'ave been one who asked me something . . . She wanted a lamb, maybe two. A blonde, with almost no boobs, big bare feet, just a bit older than me . . ."

"Was this the one?" Laviolette asked.

He quickly took out of his wallet the photo of Patricia McKetterick, taken three months before she disappeared.

"Yeees . . . maybe," the shepherd said. "She certainly 'ad those freckles on the side of 'er nose. But she looked nicer than that. 'Er clothes were more modern . . . More *in*."

"What do you mean *in*?"

"Oh!" the shepherd said, "you can't explain it . . ."

"Try."

"I dunno!" the shepherd said. "She's your daughter, isn't she?"

"She's my step-daughter. Her mother's English. She'd just come back from India . . ."

"She wanted two lambs! 'Who's going to kill 'em for you?' I asked her. 'I don't want to kill them! I want to save them! All you can think of is killing! All you can think of is money! Eating meat is murder!' 'No, they're not mine,' I told her. Then she offered me . . . She offered me . . . !"

He clasped his hands over the top of his stick at the thought of those enticing offers.

"She offered me anything. Filthy things! Then she grabbed 'er long dress in both 'ands and lifted it above 'er navel, and she wasn't wearing any knickers!"

The thought of it still made his eyes bulge.

"Only what could I do," he sighed, "with a mother like mine . . ."

"Ah! Yes, of course, when you have a mother . . .", Laviolette sighed with him.

"Oh! Mine isn't a real one!" the shepherd hissed

"Oh God!" Laviolette thought. "Now he's off! He's going to tell me his life story!"

At the risk of destroying the confidence that the angry shepherd was sharing with him, the superintendent cut him short.

"And when did that happen?"

The shepherd, whose thoughts were flying towards his mother, took a few moments to get back to the subject in hand.

"Oh! When did that 'appen?" he repeated. "That 'appened in November, maybe the 11th . . . She said to me, 'I haven't got any money. I'm offering myself! I'm worth it, you'll see. You've heard about English girls, haven't you?' But what could I do . . . with my mother . . . Then she said, 'Wait! Wait for four days! I'll have some money in four days' time.' I said again that I'd ask my boss. 'No!' she shouted, 'not the boss. They're all the same. If she knows it's to save them, she'll sell them to the butcher, even more cheaply. In four days, I'll have some cash. I'll give it to you. And me with it! You'll see what I've learned!" But what could I do, since my mother . . ."

"And when did you see her again?" Laviolette asked.

"Never!" the shepherd exclaimed. "That was the first and last time I ever saw her. And," he added, "I still think of it . . . Because if I'd really thought about it . . . Even remembering my mother . . ."

X

A WEEK BEFORE CHRISTMAS, BETWEEN SATURDAY NIGHT
and Sunday morning, events started to move fast.

Things had been getting worse for the last two or three days.
Unleashed by the usual depression, bursts of stormy weather descended
on us and were then dispersed in the force of the mistral.

On that night, the wind blew hard to the west. Snow flowed down
from the Lure mountains through all the sheltered cuttings, the Le
Deffens woods, the Calavon gap, the cliffs at Le Crau and Bane. It
descended like a waving banner on all the valleys. It flowed horizon-
tally, stuck to the fronts of houses, filled up the mouldings under the
eaves from below, blocked out the black face of the town clock. The
three old lady volunteers and the priest, who were putting the finishing
touches on the crib, had great difficulty staggering home, swathed up
to their eyes in big woollen scarves.

Where there was no obstacle in its path, the snow did not stay on
roofs or on the ground. It stuck to the west side of tree trunks and
against little bridges. Where roads were hemmed in by embankments
on both sides, all trace of them was obliterated.

In Banon, however, people thought that they would have a nice
quiet night, thanks to the storm. They only had to raise the

temperature a little in the oil heaters and stoves and just let the wind blow.

Claire stared wide-eyed as she followed the progress of the storm through her window at the Hôtel des Fraches. It was heart-wrenching to watch poor Mambo shivering as he lay curled up against the hollow trunk of a tree in the square. In the waving curtain of snow between herself and the dog she had deliberately abandoned, the same vision kept appearing: it was Jeremy's tall body rising slowly and about to twist round towards her if she didn't finish him off.

As she stared at the unbearable sight, her fists were so tightly clenched that her fingernails dug into her flesh.

She turned away and walked to the bed, where the letter from the family solicitor lay. She knew it almost by heart.

". . . Of course, this long lack of participation by your brother, who is cosignatory to any important decision, is very prejudicial to the business in hand . . . I do not doubt that you will find him soon, as you intimate in your letter, but it would be most unfortunate if, in the meantime – forgive me for mentioning it – he should be involved in some fatal mishap, for things would then stagnate until – please forgive me once again – we could produce the testator . . ."

He ended his letter by saying:

"In any case, these responsibilities seem to me to be too heavy for you to bear, and also for Jeremy, who is so unstable . . . And, should the need arise, may I give you this fatherly advice: it seems to me that Europlast's generous and profitable offer deserves your closest attention . . ."

Claire crumpled up the letter and threw it into a corner of the room. "Of course," she said to herself, "'my closest attention'. As for his fatherly advice, he'll pocket a huge commission for it."

But that wasn't the most serious aspect of the letter. "Produce the testator". She hadn't thought of that . . . When would Jeremy's body be found, lying where it was now? Her own cleverness had snapped back like a mousetrap and caught her.

*

Also looking out a window, Rosemonde and Laviolette stood close together watching the storm surging down from the heights of Banon. It shot into the town gate like an arrow, and was spewed out again under the streetlights like a triumphant geyser. The swirling wind caught the snow and sent it up towards the sky before sucking it down to the street again, where it whistled along at almost 100 kilometres an hour.

"How about a little glass of something strong?"

"It seems to me, in weather like this . . ."

"No-one will come. Their wives must have said to them, 'You're surely not going out to play cards in weather like this? Are you as anxious as all that to see Rosemonde?'"

She sat down opposite him. He began to roll a cigarette. They were alone, the two of them; almost intimate. Or at least, they were both feeling the misfortune of growing old, so they instinctively understood each other. They exchanged confidences and talked about the past until midnight. They were more and more alone. They looked deep into each other's eyes from deep in their hearts. They were up to their third little glass to give themselves courage.

The weather was too cold and too hostile for two people not to be irresistibly drawn together, given the opportunity. But they were both too afraid that all they could offer were memories. At half past midnight, they went to bed; to their separate rooms. But because they hadn't been able to, because they hadn't dared to, despite wanting to so badly, their knees trembled under them as if they were a couple of eighteen-year-olds.

Then the events of the night began.

First of all, a rusty old jalopy bumping along on its chained wheels was seen suddenly emerging from the side of a hill whose contours were invisible in the dim light that still managed to penetrate the storm. The rattletrap followed a road known only to its driver. It had uneven headlights, a broken brake light, a back mudguard held together on one side with a piece of thick wire. Nevertheless, on it went into the squall, its wipers clearing scarcely twenty centimetres of the snow sticking to the windscreen. For someone seeking solitude, it would seem to be the best night in the world. But . . .

Two spotty sixteen-year-old youths, mad about the cinema, came out of the Lido with their heads full of trucks on fire, and found themselves at midnight on the street in Manosque on what was a perfect night for a car rally.

What should they do? Go home? To the smelly oil heater and the elder sister who shamelessly pleasured herself behind the thin wall? Besides, tomorrow was Sunday . . .

They went up towards the wealthy Résidences des Prés to see what they could find. They walked almost doubled over in their thin jackets and plastic shoes. Hands deep in pockets, they fiddled with a bunch of paper-clips of various sizes and those lengths of electrical wire so useful for jump-starting a car.

One of them suddenly stopped the other to point out something in the storm. Three metres from a lamp post was an old Renault 12, painted with black and white squares, and expertly modified for racing. This was obvious from its painted signs, its pennants, its racing wheels, the number of its headlights, and the host of stickers on its windows.

Kneeling on the frozen ground, as the snow was blown away by the wind·here too, they were as patient as angels as they broke into the car door. It only took ten minutes and five more to disarm the alarm with a cleverly bent paper-clip. This was their fifth successful attempt; they were no beginners. They usually hitchhiked back home when the petrol tank gave out some thirty or fifty kilometres from Manosque. But this time – a real stroke of luck! The tank was full.

They had been thinking for quite some time of trying to do a really good endurance circuit through Forcalquier, Banon, Sault and the Méouge valley. Now was the time! The engine roared, and they took off at full speed.

Meanwhile, at Bonniol's in Revest-du-Bion, the five Seringueiros from Forcalquier, who had been playing for the Senior Citizens' Dance, were loading the drum kit into the back of the station-wagon, downing a last quick drink, and resisting the exhortations of the organisers.

"Surely you're not going out on the roads in this weather! The first snowdrifts will be forming in an hour from now, maybe less! Don't you like it here? Do stay! We can put you up."

"No, no! We've got studded tyres. Thanks all the same. Thanks for offering, but we must get back – and before the snowdrifts!"

One had a young wife, the second, a rotten cold; the other three had been on a binge for four nights straight. If you gave them a shove, they'd fall flat on their faces. And tomorrow they were performing after-noon and evening in Peyruis.

"No, no! See you next time!"

People shook their heads as they watched the red tail-light disap-pear around the church corner, to the howling curse of the wind in the branches of Sully's elm beating the air madly like archangels' wings.

Meanwhile, the old car was approaching the main square in Banon at twenty kilometres an hour. It coughed a bit between the Hôtel de Lure and the Martin pharmacy, then headed down the last descent towards the Simiane road.

The storm swept down the roadway in white swirls, breaking up as they crunched against the windscreen wipers, which skidded on the frost. The driver at the wheel had his face right up against the glass; he couldn't recognise his own countryside. The weak, badly aligned head-lights showed him trees swollen with snow, walls that looked as if they had been resurfaced from to top to bottom with a white sticky layer that blocked up windows and raised levels, making the buildings look bigger and out of shape. He had to identify the landmarks out loud.

"Those must be Calut's almond trees ... This here, Jean Laine's cabin. Ah! There's César Blanc's house 'La Rabassière'!"

Suddenly, he hit the brakes. He'd left too late! There was the first snowdrift of the night up ahead of him, forming a triangle from the bottom to the top of the embankments, blocking his way. If he drove into it, even with his chains, he'd be stuck, good and proper. According to his very rough estimation, there was still a kilometre between him and his destination. No . . . No, he'd never make it on foot. He couldn't take the chance . . .

He quickly made up his mind. Although he had the road to himself, he made several manoeuvres to turn the vehicle around towards Banon. The weird sound of the chains grinding on the asphalt lingered in the air.

Meanwhile, the Seringueiros' station-wagon crossed the tracks of the jalopy on the Banon town square.

"You should put on your seat belt!" the driver said to the drummer of the band for the third time.

"Come off it! What chance is there of seeing a gendarme at this time of night in this weather?"

He looked up at the front of the Hôtel des Fraches, where there was a light in one of the windows. He caught a fleeting glimpse of a beautiful woman's face gazing out into the dark, screened from something slightly mysterious. The memory of that beauty occupied his mind with quiet speculation for the three kilometres he still had to live.

Meanwhile, swerving from one patch of ice to another, and just missing the wall of a bridge or a tree trunk glowing with warning lights, the two youths were wild with excitement as they drove at 120 k.p.h. They couldn't see anything. There was a tunnel of snow level with the bonnet. That was the best thing yet! It was better than in the films . . . And it was all real . . . Their only regret was that no-one was there to see them.

By the time they reached the Mures Basses bend, death had already just missed mowing them down three times. They had heard the blade of his scythe whistling above their heads, and it thrilled them mightily.

Everyone knows that bend. It's a reverse turn beneath Les Ferrières, to the north of Les Plaines, and at the end of a long straight stretch where the youths had driven the Renault at full speed. As their headlights could not penetrate the darkness beyond thirty metres, they had a picture in their minds of a road that was empty; an open road that belonged to them.

Full of confidence, they went into the cutting against the left-hand embankment at 100 k.p.h. The Seringueiros' station-wagon suddenly appeared out of nowhere, headlights on full beam, about six metres ahead of them, well to the right.

The ice on the road could have saved them all. The Renault went into a skid to the right when it hit a mound of ice on the roadway, which left the way clear for the station-wagon. But seeing himself in the path of that comet, the driver instinctively tried to save himself by pulling the car over to the left.

The collision occurred in the middle of the road.

The Renault whirled round, all its door wide open. It turned over six times, humming like a top. At the second turn it ejected the passenger, who ricocheted for twelve metres, ploughing up the earth before coming to a stop, minus nose and ears, in the box bushes on the embankment, where he lay on his stomach, still quivering. The driver was hurled out on the fourth turn, hitting the empty trough of a Highways Department fountain, where he smashed his head.

With its steering destroyed, the station-wagon headed straight for Zorne's oak tree, which is used as a landmark by the army. On impact, the car burst open like a ripe melon. The roof was projected six metres into the air; the doors came crashing down like a house of cards; the passenger in the front seat was killed on impact, and slid into the snow; the dying driver stayed pinned to the steering wheel. The three others in the back crawled out on their more or less broken limbs, as far as possible from the leaking petrol tank. The big drum with all its shiny new copper trappings was thrown into the air, falling back on to the roadway, where it danced, then limped grotesquely, pushed this way and that by the storm, rolling over and over on its side like a child's hoop. It leaned over on its clattering cymbals, then on its bent triangle. With every turn, the kick pedal hit the skin of the drum with a muffled boom.

The instrument finally came to rest, some time later, in a road mender's ditch. But the storm continued to beat its torn skins and whisk over the twisted cymbals, which still vibrated as they did under the light hand that would never touch them again.

Someone in the hamlet of Largue, who was sleeping with his shutters open, was awoken by the blinding light of a petrol tank exploding. Sitting up in bed, he saw the storm in front of him turn redcurrant red, as if the sun were rising through it.

He ran to the telephone.

At that moment, the old jalopy was passing the Dauban crossroads on the way back to Banon, its ghostly chains scraping the roadway where the squall had swept away the snow.

The ever-watchful driver felt immediately that the night was not promising. Below him he could see two gendarmes hurriedly getting the van out of the garage. Above him on the town terraces, windows which had been dark a while ago were now lit up, with shadows moving about behind them. As he was about to reach the top of the road at the fountain corner, then go down the hill, lights went on in front of him. Someone was opening the big door, and Martel the mechanic's workshop lit up also, showing the breakdown lorry permanently parked outside. The driver of the old rattletrap couldn't take the only road possible in front of those men and those lights. He turned right round towards the square, but as he approached the station through the waving plumes of snow, he caught sight of the gleaming brass helmet on the head of Jules Bec, who was hurrying off, fastening his belt over his fat belly. He had just enough time to turn once again to avoid Biscarle, who was going up the steps beside the Post Office.

Curtains were being drawn. The jalopy was caught like a rat in a trap in the midst of this growing panic. The driver saw the broad, black entrance to the huge coach house at the back of the Hôtel des Fraches. He drove into it as fast as he could, turned off the engine, turned off the headlights, and lay low.

Footsteps could be heard outside on the frozen pavement. With siren blaring, the first contingent of volunteers set off on the big fire engine. The narrow beams from the headlights swept throughout the coach house, even showing up the bits of old spider webs hanging from the ceiling. The man crouched down on his seat.

People were talking loudly, asking questions of all their neighbours. The baker, in slippers and vest, came out to the square smoking his fag end, to find out what was happening. Seeing the fire engine go by, he quickly took cover. The lights went on even in the house of Maître Lagardère, the solicitor, who anxiously raised a corner of his curtains. The two hotels turned the lights on in their café bars. The fat tyres of the doctor's Porsche squealed as they went round the bend, racing past the breakdown lorry, which had to take it carefully.

Laviolette hardly heard the siren, and thought that it had nothing to do with him.

The man hounded by fate, crouching deep in the shadows in his jalopy, tried to think of a way out of his predicament. Two or three people were already walking around outside, scraping their feet and coughing their chests raw over the first cigarette of the day. It would just take one of them to want a piss and decide that the dark coach house was a good place . . . He had to work quickly; decide what to do . . . He decided . . .

The alarm lasted for three hours, during which the storm was unrelenting. The brightly shining bars in the hotels drew a few tousled-headed men ejected from the marital bed by curiosity, who took advantage of this unusual night to down an unexpected glass or two. "Today is Sunday," they thought. "And just look what happened to those four. What good does it do to deny yourself?"

The word had spread that the accident had caused four fatalities.

The firemen came back at five o'clock. The intensive-care ambulance appeared first, being driven very slowly. They were bringing those who were beyond help back to the hospital morgue. The injured had been evacuated to Manosque by the Saint-Étienne Company, which had been called to assist. The gendarmes drove the last vans back into the police garage, and Martel's breakdown lorry, ablaze with sixteen flashing lights, filed past like a futuristic hearse. Suspended in the back was the musicians' station-wagon, bumping along on its buckled back wheels, minus doors and roof.

Everyone came to the hotels to cheer themselves up with a few glasses of brandy and tell each other what they knew of the nightmare accident. They were still there dragging their feet in the storm and the snow while the chorus of noises, exclamations and discussions went on until six in the morning, when the lights were finally turned off in the bars and the words of the last conversation died in the whistling wind. One by one the windows went dark. Banon would sleep late that Sunday morning.

Apart from the car wreck strung up and swinging in the wind in the back of the breakdown lorry, the one person left was the man crouching in the back of the hotel yard in his old rattletrap. It was only when he could hear no other noise than the usual hum of the baker's kneading machine that he dared start up the engine. He came out of the shadows into the squall with shoulders hunched and muscles tense, expecting to see some straggler or early waker suddenly appear on the street; someone who would recognise him and say, "Hey! What are you doing there?"

But no. Banon had had enough excitement for one night. He didn't see a soul. He shivered as he passed what was left of the station-wagon.

He bumped along on his way to the dismal sound of his chains. He was even lucky enough to see the weather change eventually when the south wind suddenly began blowing through the huge beech tree on the edge of his property.

Beneath the curtain of snow which rose without warning, revealing the constellation of the Great Bear, you could have followed the progress of that car for some time on the road sloping towards the valley, but clear of snow.

Sometimes, when he thought of the last few hours, the driver looked fixedly, with wild staring eyes, at the narrow space cleared by the windscreen wipers. After a while, his right hand let go of the steering wheel, and he kept it pressed to his mouth like someone seeing his house on fire.

His solid common sense told him that the huge spanner God Almighty had just thrown into the works clearly indicated the beginning of the end.

XI

DAYLIGHT CAME WITH A WATERY SUN. THE SNOW PLOUGHS
appeared at eight o'clock, but the melting snow was streaming down
from the roofs, and they were only needed for the snowdrifts, also
beginning to melt.

When the mist lifted over Banon at about ten o'clock, the tiles gleamed
in the brilliant sunshine. You could hear the clink of pairs of bowls
knocking against each other. These belonged to certain Marseillais
already keen to measure their skill against the natives in a few mighty
games of *pétanque*. Players and spectators filled the square.

The smell of special Sunday dishes – braised wild pig and jugged
hare – began to mingle and float in the air. The baker put the four
dozen cream puffs he baked specially on Sundays into the shop window.
They were always gone in a quarter of an hour; he always promised to
make more. The Bleus, the Bayles, Biscarle, Jules Bec, and many others
who were not clients of Rosemonde's, arrived with hands behind their
backs, clean caps and cheeks shining with pumice after shaving, to get
a breath of Sunday air and comment on the night's events. Groups went
and gazed thoughtfully at the wreckage of the station-wagon, still strung
up near Martel's workshop.

At about eleven, Alyre Morelon turned up from his nearby farm through the Bonnes Rues short-cut, holding a freshly-brushed Roseline on a lead. Roseline loved noise and people, and Alyre was so fond of his sow that on Sundays like this one, he took her to the town square to watch the games of bowls. The men laughed at first, but when they learned that Roseline could root out six kilos of truffles a day, this hard-working animal enjoyed a certain respect. And to Alyre's great pride, some even bent down to scratch her head.

But this particular morning, Roseline was in a fretful mood. She grunted more and more loudly, pulling on her lead in the direction of the Hôtel des Fraches. Was it towards the smell of the wild suckling pig, or was it the hare?

When the games moved from one end of the square to the other, the spectators followed them and stood once more in a curved line around them. Everyone concentrated on the shots that were about to be bowled; except one who stood with his hands behind his back, fidgeting incessantly as he cast furtive looks in the direction of the coach house behind the Hôtel des Fraches. Alyre went up to greet him. But when he held out his hand, Roseline shrieked so loud and long that the champion bowler who was taking aim at that moment missed his shot and swore horribly.

"For heaven's sake, Roseline! Will you stop screaming blue murder?" Alyre said. Roseline balked with the full weight of her 180 kilos, and began her ear-splitting cries again. You couldn't do anything. It was impossible. Her calls to the crowd were driving everyone crazy. And in between these insistent shrieks, she kept trumpeting, growling and quivering from head to foot. In her case, "yelling like a stuck pig" was not just a figure of speech. The man Morelon had just greeted was looking at her with something like grim terror in his eyes. The man and the pig stared at each other with utter hostility.

The bowls players protested bitterly.

"Listen! Why don't you take her home? She'll make us miss every-thing."

That was the moment when Laviolette slipped from group to group to reach his car, which was parked among the players. The blue Mercedes was still there beside his old Vedette. He gave a perfunctory handshake to Alyre and the man next to him, then got into his car. He heard the sow shrieking its head off for some time yet.

"She really is screaming blue murder!" he thought absent-mindedly.

He was a countryman at heart, and in a place like this he felt as if he were on holiday. Besides, there was nothing much to be done at the moment. He had sent the rubbish from the drop-outs' hideout to the laboratory, together with precise instructions about what the technicians should look for, and he was waiting for the result.

XII

DRIVING AT THE SPEED OF A FUNERAL CORTEGE AS USUAL, he made his way towards Vachères and his old friend the Marquis des Brèdes, who went by the name of Jean Fréron in the Resistance because he hated Voltaire.* They had both narrowly escaped death in the Massif d'Allevard.

They had never seen each other since that marvellous time, but Brèdes was well known as an ornithologist with the Science Research Council. Laviolette received postcards sent by him from all over the world depicting extraordinary birds threatened with extinction in Tasmania or the Galapagos. The only news written on the back was: "What do you think of this one? Doesn't it remind you of someone?"; or else: "There are only 200 pairs of these left. And all the males are homosexual! Can you imagine that?"

Every one of these cards from Brèdes – he insisted on dropping the "de" – was in the same style. They had shared a warm friendship and, as soon as Laviolette telephoned him from Banon, he invited him to lunch on Sunday.

"And you live alone, I imagine?" Laviolette said.

* Fréron and Voltaire disagreed profoundly in matters of philosophy.

"I imagine you do too?" Brèdes said.

The windows with their large panes of glass looked out on an oval pond and a bare willow leaning over the still, bronze-mirror surface. It reflected the brilliant blue sky. Further away, the northern aspect of Vachères stood alone, casting a black shadow over the bare fields.

Although the room contained many beautiful pieces of furniture, it seemed empty; everything in it was on a vast scale. They had both just got up from the dinner table, where the farmer's wife had served them with an air of disapproval, as there was no tablecloth. She felt obliged to point out that, despite appearances, there was no lack of table linen in the house.

"I can't get her to understand that I like to see the reflection of the china and the bottles in the polished wood. You see this Saint-Emilion that we've just drunk? Well, it gives me as much pleasure – of another kind, of course, but similar – to see the image of the bottle and its label upside down in the wood of this table . . ."

He lit his pipe from the embers in the hearth. A thin man with long legs, he moved very quickly and silently, giving the impression of hardly touching the ground.

"I'm telling you these things, because I think you understand them . . ." Brèdes concluded.

Laviolette nodded his head. Warped beams and old doors creaked around him. The house was topped with a huge double-pitched roof over two floors of unused rooms. The echoing empty rooms, each with a fireplace and red hexagonal tiles on the floor but never any furniture, created a kind of mystery surrounding the walls.

The ancestral home of the Brèdes was never a château, but a silk-worm house. Fifty years after the last harvest there, the smell of silk-worms spinning their cocoons still lingered in dark corners of the corridors.

"So, what exactly brings you to Banon?" Brèdes asked. "If it's not confidential?"

"No. It's not confidential. It's simply a mystery! Five disappear-ances . . ."

"Of whom?"

"Hippies!"

"Oh! Them! I've come across them as far away as the shores of Lake Kukunor. You're pretty good if you can tell where they'll appear and disappear! And why!"

"Maybe so . . . But in this case, it does seem that . . . Everything points to them coming to Banon and staying there."

"And no-one can find them?"

"No."

"How long has this been going on?"

"The earliest one was reported four months ago."

"And you were sent here for that? Can't the gendarmes deal with it?"

Laviolette sighed. "The people who have disappeared nearly all have foreign names. Those in high places don't like so many foreigners suddenly disappearing. And people mustn't start to panic . . . So, I was approached. You're unremarkable, you'll do for any job, they told me, and you're from the Basses-Alpes as well . . .

"But enough of that!" Laviolette continued. "You were fairly smart in the old days, and you have a logical mind. Can you think of any reason why five vagabonds with nothing to connect them – apart from the fact that they were hippies and poor as church mice, by choice or by necessity – can you think of a single reason why they should disappear specifically in Banon?"

"In Banon? Are you sure?"

"I wasn't at first, but the facts are piling up, and being guided by those facts, I repeat that it's likely. But I still come up against this un-answered question: for what reason? That's why I'm asking if you can think of one."

Brèdes thought hard, staring into the fire as he smoked his pipe.

"Are they all the same sex?" he asked.

"Three men and two women."

"Age?"

"All young. Between twenty and twenty-five."

"Have you looked everywhere? In all the hospitals in the area?

In institutions? In the religious communities? In worker's co-operatives?"

"Everywhere," Laviolette said. "You know that the gendarmes are very efficient in this kind of work."

"And not one has been found? Dead or alive?"

"Dead or alive. You know that they don't give up easily around here. It's on the gendarmes' agenda, and every time they question anyone in the area, they always ask and show the photos."

"In my opinion," Brèdes said, "they're dead."

"All five of them? Young and apparently in good health?"

"If you're fairly sure that they haven't left, that's the only answer I can see. How could anyone disappear in Banon and still be alive? Nine hundred inhabitants! There are thousands of hectares of bare land. Shepherds, hunters, poachers, walkers, gendarmes, helicopters. No. In Banon? Alive? Impossible! Either they've left or they're dead."

"No. They haven't left."

"Then they're dead."

"But why, if that's the case?"

"Ah!" Brèdes said. "I'm afraid I can't help you there. I haven't a crystal ball. You mentioned me being smart a moment ago. In those days I flattered myself that I was not unobservant. Well, my friend, times have changed. For six months now I've been racking my brains over a small personal problem that I can't seem to solve."

"Go ahead . . . I'm at your service. Tell me about it."

"Oh! It's stupid really. Come on into the library. The drinks are there and the farmer's wife can clear up and be on her way. It's Sunday. I don't want to keep her here for too long . . ."

They went through a low door in a thick wall. The library was more intimate that the living room. There were bird of paradise feathers lying on the covers of books scattered about on little tables. The shelves held books of all kinds. Paperbacks and bound books were mixed up together – the clutter of a real reader. They had to clear two chairs in front of the hearth to sit down.

"Well now," Laviolette said, as he rolled a cigarette, "what's this mystery?"

Brèdes turned on his cane chair and pointed to a small article of furniture in front of a window.

"Do you see that bookstand?"

"The craftsman who made it must have enjoyed his work," Laviolette said. "Look at that piece of wood!"

My father bought it years ago from Bébé Fabre, the antique dealer in Manosque. Do you remember Bébé Fabre?"

"I can see him now!" Laviolette exclaimed. "He came to Piégut . . . I must have been about eight at the time . . . My grandfather sold him his grandfather's clock. I can still see him, with his pince-nez, his hat, his buff-coloured cotton trousers . . ."

"And the cape that hardly reached down to his watch-chain!"

They both laughed. They were in fact ten years old when this man, long since dead, looked like the person they had just described.

"Well now," Brèdes continued, "this bookstand usually held a very old book . . . A book published in sixteen hundred and something, containing all kinds of old wives' recipes and formulas. Right . . . Every year when I'm here for Easter or Whitsun, I give a reception for the war veterans of Banon, Vachères and Revest. Oh, they don't all come. There are some who make a point of not coming because of my title! It's a family tradition. My father used to do it, and I enjoy it too. It's an opportunity to see the people of the region again, to talk . . . We all speak the local dialect. We cook one or two lambs on a spit . . . You know the sort of thing I mean. And we drink! I don't bring out my best wine, but I still offer them something reasonably good. Well, as there are usually about sixty of us on the day, I open the three doors. That gives me three rooms opening into each other: the drawing room, which we never use, the living room and the library. Right!"

He got up and walked around the table piled with books and an unfinished manuscript. He lit his pipe again, as it had gone out while he was talking.

"On that day, the weather was bad – stormy, almost dark. The brandy and liqueurs are usually served outside on the rows of stone seats under the chestnut trees. But this time it was out of the question. We stayed inside talking. A few men were standing around the bookstand consulting this old book. I thought it would amuse them if I read, or rather translated – since it's in 17th-century French – a few witch stories, which made them laugh. After that I moved from group to group, taking part in the conversation, talking about various people: those who had died, the womanisers, the deceived husbands . . . About everything really. After five o'clock the numbers began to thin out, as always happens in gatherings. You know: there are even some who leave without saying goodbye to you. Nobody pays any attention.

"At seven o'clock I was alone, with the farmer's wife, her two daughters and all the mess to clear up. The four of us set to . . . and it was the farmer's wife who pointed it out to me. A worthy soul, but she's from Le Queyras, and doesn't like us much. There's no crucifix over the head of my bed, so I'm a marked man! She's never got used to it. And my sixty guests: she despises them because they're peasants, although she's one herself. She's the one who shouted to me, 'They've stolen your book!' She usually gave it a wide berth. 'It's witchcraft,' she would say. 'You should throw it in the fire!' I was rather worried, as I knew I had left it on the bookstand, but I didn't want to agree entirely with her. Besides, was I really sure? Can one ever be sure of anything? So I said to the woman, 'No! It's not that! I've put it somewhere else. It must be in all that stuff lying about on the tables. Now don't worry. I'll look for it tomorrow.' I did look. To put my mind at rest . . . but . . ."

He made a face.

"I've never found it."

"Could your book fit into someone's pocket?"

"Oh, yes. It was roughly 12 x 20 centimetres . . ."

"Is it worth any money?"

"Ah, well. I haven't finished telling you the story. My father found it under the desk part of the bookstand that Bébé Fabre sold him. And when my father subsequently pointed this out and offered to pay, old Fabre – who was honesty itself – said no, it was his fault; he should have looked more closely at what he was selling. He wouldn't accept a penny. That would be a lesson to him! And besides, he had another copy in his own library . . ."

"So you don't know if the book is worth anything?"

"What I do know is that my father, who knew the value of things, had four truffles sent to Bébé Fabre every Christmas."

A faint ringing sound came from the depths of the house.

"Would that be the telephone?" Laviolette asked.

"That's right," Brèdes sighed. "I'm waiting on some pathology results. A very nasty virus is decimating the birds to the south of Punta Arenas. The telephone is in my office."

"I'll let you go and answer it."

"No, no. Come with me. It's not confidential."

There was a smell of cold pipe in the office, with subtle olfactory overtones emanating from floor to ceiling.

Brèdes picked up the receiver.

"Believe it or not, it's for you!" he said, much surprised.

"For me?" Laviolette said. "Who is it?"

He remembered having told Rosemonde that he was lunching with the Marquis de Brèdes. He listened to the person on the line without showing any reaction.

"Right," he said. "I'm coming."

He looked at Brèdes, who did not question him.

"My friend," he said, "I'm afraid I'll have to cut my visit short. It was the chief gendarme. They've just discovered a murder. May I use your phone?"

"Of course."

Laviolette called the special police services in Marseilles, as he was authorised to do if need be, to request assistance from the forensic team from the Criminal Records Office.

"To Banon! Banon! Yes, that's right. And smartly! Tell them to use the siren if necessary."

He hung up and put out his hand.

"I'm sorry, old man. As you can see, duty calls . . ."

"One of your missing persons?"

"I don't know yet. Possibly . . ."

"Can we meet again?"

"I'll get in touch with you as soon as I can. As far as your book is concerned . . . As you can see, I don't have time to help you."

Brèdes laughed. "Oh! It's not as important as all that. I can live quite well without it."

XIII

AT MIDDAY, SUNDAY IN BANON WAS AT ITS HEIGHT. ENCOURA-ged to go out by the fine weather, people from Forcalquier, Manosque and Apt, who were on the road at the time, found themselves in Banon.

"What about stopping here for lunch?"

For the two hotels, Le Lure and Les Fraches, there was a lunch-time rush every Sunday. As well as that, a big advance booking took up one whole room. They were the fifty guests at a wedding celebrated the evening before at Lardiers, and Banon had been chosen for the reception. Six ornamental cakes placed among the white carnations graced the impeccable white table linen.

There was frantic activity in the kitchen. Twenty-five customers were already installed at small tables and, at half past twelve, the fourteen wedding cars arrived, sounding their horns. They parked in the square in orderly fashion, then fifty hungry people rushed to the tables, pushing and shoving to be the first seated. The bride's train was rather muddy because, when they came out of the church, the evening before, they had to cross the threshold several times to please the photographers. The train, held by careless little boys, had ended up as a cleaning cloth for the melting snow on the forecourt.

But what did that matter. Everyone was now sitting with forks in hand and a Basses-Alpes peasant's hunger to be satisfied. Some had already fortified themselves with preliminary glasses of pastis; two or three of the uncles hadn't sobered up since the night before.

Four waitresses whirled around the guests.

"Whatever you do, don't turn anyone away."

If necessary they would put people in the café. Apart from the summer trade, Sunday was the only opportunity to make a bit of money . . .

The owner's wife and her sister took down the orders. Three extras served the wedding party. The owner, in a state of panic at his over-loaded stoves, inundated his underlings with contradictory orders. Little by little, however, everything fell into place and order reigned once more. The kitchen hummed along busily as it did every week, amid the clattering of plates being emptied at top speed. The two people washing up were sweating over their sinks.

By half past one, six bills had already been settled. There was still enough to feed a few latecomers, if need be.

The owner opened the big refrigerator to check how much he had in reserve.

"God Almighty! Marie-Jeanne! I'm going to run out of *vacherin* ices. There's only one left, and there are already two ordered for the eight people on table four. Georgette! Run to the storeroom and get me six *vacherins.*"

Georgette the waitress was his niece – a plump eighteen-year-old in flamingo-pink tights. For the moment she was doing a great job squeezing her bottom between the backs of the guests, who were seated too close together. The owner's wife came to stand in for her.

"Run to the storeroom, Georgette. Don't upset your uncle. He's in a filthy mood!"

Georgette hurried out of the restaurant and went into the huge store-room. The extra provisions were at the back in a very large freezer with a four cubic metre capacity and sides decorated with two blue ice crys-tals. They had not been able to put the freezer inside because of its size and its noisy compressor, which would have disturbed the customers. It held everything: ice creams, beans, unskinned hares, and even one or two wild boar, "just in case', i.e. if local production was insufficient.

Georgette put out a brawny arm and with a quick jerk, opened the lid.

"What on earth can Georgette be doing with those *vacherins*?" the owner exclaimed. "Pierrot, find out what she's up to, and get her back here."

Pierrot was a pimply kitchen hand who was going to hotel school. During the holidays, his parents sent him to work with a colleague to earn a bit of money. He went off at the double.

What he saw in the gloom stopped him in his tracks. There at the far end of the room straight in front of him, and literally bent in two, was Georgette with the top half of her body completely buried in the freezer, thus revealing the entire contents of her flamingo-pink tights under her short skirt. Pierrot could hardly believe his eyes . . . He had dreamt about girls in that position for ages as he woke in the morning, highly stimulated. He walked forward feeling weak at the knees, with his hand across his mouth, whispering repeatedly behind his fingers,

"Oh, wow! Oh, wow!"

His heart was in his mouth as he tiptoed forward so that he wouldn't scare Georgette. His fingers lightly touched the promised land. As he had a slight squint, he could ogle the girl's tights and see into the huge interior of the freezer at the same time. That was when he saw, lying on the bed of fur provided by the hares and the boars, a Hindu Brahmin staring up at him.

He collapsed beside Georgette, who had fainted.

The boss was jealous even of girls he didn't fancy himself.

"Blanche!" he called, "would you go and see what those two are up to? It seems to me they're taking a hell of a time to fetch six *vacherins*!"

Blanche was his sister-in-law: bra size 120 cms, fairly blotchy skin, feet like little boats, calves like a mountaineer. Her voice, which was naturally piercing, easily hit high C when she was excited.

She shot out of the storeroom with the speed of a cannon ball.

"There's a body!" she screamed to all and sundry in the square.

"Help! There's a body in the freezer!"

She rushed to the kitchen, collapsed against the table, sobbing over the parsley on the chopping-board.

"Oh, Paul! It can't be! Here! On a Sunday! A body! In the freezer!" she exclaimed, her voice rising steadily in C major.

She had just realised that the freezer would have to be replaced.

The owner dashed to the telephone, but everyone else was rushing around as well.

First of all, the whole wedding party, half the other customers and all the bowls players from the square converged as they surged en masse towards the storeroom and the strange coffin.

Out of consideration, they only just left enough room for the bride to pass and get a good spot in the front row. As for the others, it was every man for himself. The fat ones pushed with their stomachs. The short ones trod on the tall ones' feet. The only people still seated were a few Marseillais, quite blasé about such excitement, who stayed sucking on the shells of their crayfish. Even four-year-old children wanted to see, and stamped their feet angrily if anyone tried to stop them. One of them managed to worm his way right up to the freezer. His head hardly reached over the top, but open-mouthed and standing on tip-toe, he didn't miss a thing. It was his first dead body.

The gendarmes were there in two minutes. It was already too late to hold back the crowd.

"Just look at that!" the constable said to his sergeant. "We'll be blamed once again for not noting the clues from the crime scene."

It was a fact that dozens of hands had held the edges of the freezer, where earlier there were perhaps only those of the person who had committed the crime. The earth floor of the storeroom, which no doubt had shown footprints made by the murderer, had since been trampled underfoot.

As soon as there were four of them, the gendarmes pushed the crowd out of the storeroom, and closed it off permanently with a chain.

Contrary to his usual practice, Laviolette drove at more than 80 kms

an hour on the road, and when he arrived there, he had some difficulty getting through the crowd. It was no use showing his pass and
asking people to make way; a gendarme had to intervene so that he
could step over the chain.

"Our apologies," the sergeant said. "The Chief won't be here until
this evening, but going by what we heard you say the other night, we
thought it best . . ."

"No, no! You did the right thing."

He went over to the freezer, which no-one had thought of switching
off. Its icy mist rose up into the shadows of the storeroom.

"Well!" Laviolette exclaimed. "At least this one's well preserved."

The man's body lay stiff as a frozen fish on his bed of rabbit fur and
pigskin, his beard as frosty as Father Christmas. He was wearing a robe
of rough Indian cotton, and his feet were at right angles in their wooden-
soled sandals. A long necklace of cypress wood beads hung down to
his navel, with a cherry-red copy of one of Robert Morel's "O Collection"
books hanging from it.

Laviolette immediately recognised the hippie who had emerged from
his sleeping bag in the Montsalier church when he arrived, and had
then immediately sunk back disdainfully into his nirvana.

Dr Lusel from Banon, who had been notified by the police, arrived
soon after. He was a young man, about twenty-five to thirty, and this
Sunday corpse absolutely amazed him.

"How long ago do you think he died?" Laviolette asked.

The young man spread his arms. "For the moment, it's impossible
to say with any accuracy. Just think of it! He's lying there at −20°. From
the look of him, I'd say he's been frozen for several hours. Only an
autopsy can . . ."

"I've sent for forensics. Is your hospital equipped to do it?"

The doctor laughed.

"For an autopsy? I should think so!"

"All right. We'll do it tomorrow. Sergeant, will you get the owner of
the hotel? No! Wait! I'll go. And don't let anyone come near here."

He went into the kitchens through the swinging door between the rubbish bins that crowded the floor, made himself known to the owner, and told him what was happening. After about a quarter of an hour, the hubbub finally died down.

It was a matter for the gendarmes, after all . . . The aroma of the jugged hare cooking on the stove rose up, filling the air. The wedding guests answered its call, went back to their places in orderly fashion, and sat with forks at the ready. As the *vacherins* were off the menu, because naturally nobody believed that the corpse hadn't lain on them, they'd just have apples for dessert. The wedding party didn't mind. Thank heavens they had the decorated cakes. The bride was delighted. When *she* talked about her marriage, she'd be able to say, "Believe it or not, on *my* wedding day . . ."

"You know, that's a lousy trick someone played on me," the owner said to Laviolette. "Now I'll have to replace the freezer. No-one will want to eat anything that comes out of it. I'll have to change the brand and . . ."

"Come on now," Laviolette said. "You'll sell it to another restaurant in Aix or the Drôme. It won't be so bad . . . When was the last time someone opened it?"

"Last night. At eight o'clock. Some officers from the base wanted crêpes Suzette."

He rolled his eyes.

"I ask you! Crêpes Suzette – in Banon! Fortunately I had some. An old packet I'd been given as a sample."

"Who went to get them?"

The owner looked over his shoulder

"My niece!"

Laviolette turned round. Sturdy Blanche, who was once again her usual formidable self, was trying to pour a spoonful of local brandy between Georgette's lips. The girl was still shivering and shaking. As Blanche had found the kitchen hand unconscious next to her daughter, but with his hand lying limply across her treasure's bottom, she had roundly slapped both their faces – apparently to stop their teeth chattering – and now she was comforting them with small spoonfuls of loaf sugar soaked in brandy, telling them off in no uncertain terms all the while.

"Miss, are you the one who discovered the . . . body?"

Georgette's complexion was usually pink and red, but she now turned the colour of an old packet of lard. She shook her head, unable to speak.

"Georgette!" Blanche roared, "Don't be such a baby. Answer the gentleman or I'll give you a clout you won't forget."

"Yes, sir . . ."

"And you're the one who went to get the crêpes Suzette yesterday evening?"

"Yes, sir . . ."

"And when you were there, did you notice anything?"

"No, sir. It was dark. I had a torch. I ran. I'm always scared in that storeroom at night . . ."

"And none of you," Laviolette said to everyone there, "had to go back to the freezer between eight o'clock last night and one o'clock today?"

"No," the owner called out from his stove, where he was standing over a paella surrounded by the fumes of frying food. "No! I get my stores in on Saturday and put them in the fridge over there. It's only when we run out, as we did today, that . . ."

"Right!" Laviolette said.

He heard something going on in the square and looked down to the end of the corridor.

It was the forensic men from Criminal Records arriving, backed up by Guyot and Leprince, two tall nonchalant police inspectors with long hair and jeans.

They introduced themselves.

"We've been told to make ourselves useful to you . . ."

"They're generous with their reinforcements," Laviolette thought. He looked at his watch. It was exactly one hour and ten minutes since he telephoned headquarters.

"Good God! Good God!" he exclaimed.

It was 120 kms from Marseilles to Banon. The team with its equipment was getting out of a Renault 5, which was almost smoking, having driven so fast through so much mud.

"Wow! We went flat out. The siren ran hot. We nearly skittled at least three old codgers driving on the left at 50 kms an hour!"

"At the risk of killing three more," Laviolette grumbled.

"Oh! By the way. Where is he? Where is he?"

They were flapping around eagerly like young roosters. Finding a body was great fun for these boys from Criminal Records. You should see the enthusiasm they put into taking the stark flash photos that make everyone else shudder, from the Director of Public Prosecutions down.

Laviolette took them to the freezer, where the sergeant and the doctor were waiting for them. The boys bustled around setting up their equipment with obvious relish.

XIV

IT WAS THE MARCH OF JUSTICE – EQUIPPED TO THE TEETH! The body was not the only thing they photographed. They shot everything: the storeroom door, the cobweb-covered ceiling, the ground trampled by countless feet, the peeling walls, the ancient "Banon–Revest-du-Bion" coach – which brought cries of disbelief – the three customers' cars, the pile of empty crates, the old set of rusty kitchen knives, a huge ring of horseshoes threaded on a piece of wire swinging like a chandelier from a hook in a beam. They didn't miss a thing; not a square centimetre of the place where the body was discovered.

"Fingerprints?"

Laviolette raised his eyebrows.

"Go ahead and try, but . . ."

"What could we do?" the sergeant said. "By the time we arrived, maybe three minutes after we were called, there were about a hundred people here."

"No-one can do the impossible," Laviolette said.

"However," the doctor added, "I can tell you how he died . . ."

"Go ahead."

They both leaned over the body. The beard, which was stiff with frost, bent up like a hinge when it was moved.

"Look!" the doctor said.

He was pointing to the dead man's throat, or what was left of it. It had been cut from ear to ear, so widely that the edges of the wound had not closed and the flesh inside, which was solid with cold, looked like a dark little cave of rose-red meat.

"But one thing is certain," the doctor observed. "The man wasn't killed here. There's not a drop of blood."

"So he must have been brought here?"

The doctor made a gesture indicating that he didn't know.

Criminal Records would work on that.

Inspector Laviolette gazed at the dead man who had nothing: no hope and no past; only freedom. Who could possibly have anything against someone so physically and mentally destitute?

He had in his gloved hands the book from the "O Collection" attached to the string of wooden beads by a ring. The boys had just found some fingerprints on it. It was a philosophical handbook of protest against the death penalty; a kind of breviary, a rosary to be told for all occasions. Each page contained a maxim:

"We are all murderers! A murderer is a sick person, who should be treated, not put down! Capitalism kills murderers to please the bourgeoisie! Let us take pity on murderers! Today's murderer is tomorrow's decent man!" etc.

"The ambulance is outside," the sergeant said. "Have you finished?"

"More or less. You can take him away . . ."

"Is there a morgue at the hospital? Dr Rabinovitch won't be there until tomorrow."

"Something that serves as one, in any case."

Laviolette looked into the shadows at the big body of the old coach with a great feeling of nostalgia. He would love to have sat in it for a ride to Revest-du-Bion . . .

"On a Sunday afternoon, to boot!" he suddenly exclaimed. "And they want us to take pity on them!"

He went off with the sergeant to the police station, where he made several phone calls. The chief appeared as he was putting down the receiver, very disappointed to have missed it all. He and his wife had gone to lunch with the chief gendarme at Forcalquier. He couldn't get over the news.

"Are you going to investigate this case?" he asked Laviolette.

"I'm awaiting instructions . . . Don't forget that I'm here to make enquiries about a certain number of missing persons, but there is nothing to indicate a priori that this murder is connected to them. Nevertheless . . ."

He told him that he had seen the victim alive three days ago at Montsalier.

"For the moment, the two young inspectors who were sent to assist me are questioning the hotel staff and guests, while your men are going around the area to collect any possible information. It seems that the murder wasn't committed in the storeroom. The body was moved there."

"In the meantime," the chief said, "I'll send two men to Montsalier to sort out everyone they find up there, and bring them back here, handcuffed if necessary. This time, it's murder."

"Just a moment!" Laviolette said.

He called down the corridor. He asked the Criminal Records people, who were packing up to leave, to develop two photos of the body straight away, so that they could be shown to the hippies who were brought back.

He turned round again and sat down.

"Obviously he had nothing on him?"

"Nothing! An American shirt, two pairs of long johns, one over the other, ski tights over those, the wooden-soled sandals and the Indian cotton robe."

"No papers? No tobacco or cigarettes?"

"Where would he have put them? He had no pockets!"

At that moment they heard steps in the corridor. Two gendarmes were encouraging two strapping, ruddy-faced men to go in, ignoring their protestations that "really, they didn't want to disturb . . ."

"Not at all! Not at all! You're not disturbing us. Come in. Sit down. Here, the chief will take your statement."

"Well, you know . . . We haven't got much to tell. Is it really worth interrupting you?"

The gendarmes gently urged the stone-cutter and the petrol station attendant forward.

Hardly had they set foot in the police station than the rumour already circulated that Jules Bec and Absalon Biscarle had killed the hippie to rape him. Their frantic wives came running to find out. They had to be restrained, reassured, convinced that the rumour was false . . .

"Now. Just what did you see?" the chief asked.

Laviolette sat in the background, rolling a cigarette.

"Not much," Jules Bec said.

They had accommodated his 110 kilos and huge thighs on a chair as best they could. This shy man with his large head was so overcome at being in a gendarme's office that he dripped with sweat.

"Just tell the chief," the sergeant said encouragingly, "what you said at Rosemonde Burle's."

"I was just leaving home," Jules Bec said. "I'm a fireman, you know. The siren sounded. The weather was awful! The wind and snow were blowing everywhere! They stung my eyes like needles. Suddenly I was blinded by the headlights of a car. I saw something further away in the falling snow . . . something that stopped, backs and turns under the plane trees. It made a strange noise . . ."

"Could you make out what kind of car it was?"

Jules Bec, with a doubtful look on his face, took a good minute wiping his brow and breathing hard before he spoke.

"Perhaps it was a Beetle," he said at last. "A Mini Cooper? Or maybe a 4 CV? It's hard to say. I don't know if you remember what a dreadful night it was . . . But it seemed to me . . ."

"Yes?" the chief said patiently.

"It seemed to me that it wanted to avoid me."

Phew! He'd said it . . . It's always so hard to express a personal opinion. Absalon Biscarle, on the other hand, was quite the opposite. He'd been fidgeting and opening his mouth to speak for the last five minutes. The other gendarme had trouble keeping him in check.

"Wait! You'll have your turn to speak."

Tiny Biscarle was as sure and resolute as huge Jules Bec was shy and hesitating.

"I know! I can tell you! I was going up the steps. It was just as I reached the top that the headlights blinded me. But I was looking at street level. I saw it! I'm sure it was a Beetle! Yes, I'm sure of it. It was white, squat, solid. It was a Beetle for sure! And I thought so too, Jules. I thought that it wanted to avoid me."

"I don't suppose it would be any use asking you if you saw who was driving?"

"What! Saw who was driving. You ask us if we saw who was driving? On a night like that? And we were hurrying off to do our job as firemen. What time did we have?"

"And," Jules Bec added, "do you remember the noise it made?"

"A ghostly noise!" exclaimed Biscarle. "Catalac . . . Catalac . . . Catalaca . . ."

"Of chains?" Laviolette suggested.

"That's it! Chains."

"And you lost sight of it immediately?"

"Just like that!" Biscarle said.

"As if by magic!" Jules Bec said. "But on a night like that, it's not surprising. And besides, we didn't have any time or reason to wonder what had become of it. As for me, I had hardly woken up properly. I was buckling my belt."

One of the gendarmes joined in.

"If I may . . ." he said.

"Go ahead! Go ahead!" the chief said.

"When we took the statements of these two witnesses, before bringing them to you, we questioned everyone who was up at that time: the baker and Eugène Martel, who we woke up with our telephone call. He was getting his breakdown lorry out at the time. No-one saw the car. And yet it must have done a U-turn, as they seem to be saying. The only way it could have gone passed by Martel's garage. He would have seen it . . ."

"Therefore," the sergeant said, "it can't have left Banon at that time?"

"Therefore," Laviolette said, "it could easily have ducked into the coach house . . ."

"Are we still needed?" Jules Bec asked.

"No. Not for the moment. You can make your written statement tomorrow morning. You can leave now. Thank you. Go and get some rest. You've earned it, after a night like that."

At that moment, the terrible screech of a stuck pig suddenly rent the air of the Esplanade and Alyre Morelon rushed in, holding in his arms the same muddy little dachshund that Laviolette recognised as the one he had tried to catch in the square. Roseline preceded him, making a noise that was more piercing than a siren.

A gendarme had gone over to block the doorway, but just you try to restrain a man in a state and a sow that weighs 180 kilos! Both of them burst in, to the stunned surprise of the chief and Laviolette. Alyre sank on to the chair that was still warm from Jules Bec. The exhausted sow collapsed in a heap on the floor. The typewriter and the picture of the President of the Republic shook with the impact. A cloud of smoke was forced back into the oil stove.

"I'm worn out!" Alyre proclaimed. "I've been running like mad. Roseline's tired out. Give Roseline some water! She's the one. She's found it. And give the dog something to eat. It's starving."

He handed the dachshund over to a gendarme, but it was Laviolette who took it, held it against him and didn't let go.

"That's it!" Alyre exclaimed. "That's what's been bothering me since autumn. That's what I wanted to say but didn't because I was afraid I'd be taken for a real idiot. That was it!"

He drew out of his pocket the scapular of wooden beads that he had found earlier among the dead leaves, and threw it on the table.

The whole company, apart from the two men who had left to find the hippies at Montsalier, gathered around this man who was trying to say too many things at once. Someone, however, did go and get a basin of water for the pig.

"Don't panic!" the chief said. "Alyre, calm down . . ."

"I feel sick. My nose took more than if I was stabbed by a knife. And Roseline! I hope it hasn't ruined her sense of smell."

They had to wait another three full minutes of snuffling, blowing loudly into a handkerchief and fending off invisible flies, before Alyre Morelon was able to explain to the gendarmes and Laviolette what had caused his agitation.

Laviolette whistled while Alyre regained his composure with a little glass of brandy that a gendarme fetched for him.

In the middle of Alyre's story, he shouted, "Just a minute!" And he sent someone to see if the team from Criminal Records had left by now.

"A good half-hour ago."

They must have already got as far as Pertuis, with the help of their siren. An odd surprise awaited them when they arrived in the form of a message just received: "Come back to Banon with heavy equipment."

"This time," Laviolette said, "I think it's too big a deal for me to continue acting as a substitute for the Department of Public Prosecutions. I must get a message to Digne."

"I was just about to suggest the same thing," the chief said.

XV

GEORGETTE HAD FAINTED IN FRONT OF THE FREEZER AT about 1.30 in the afternoon.

The dachshund Mambo, chased away everywhere and dazed with hunger, cold and fatigue, turned his back on the town at about 1.15, and wandered on to the first road that presented itself. Quite alone in the world, he whimpered as he slowly made his way along the bank at the side of the road, head drooping and nose to the ground. Occasionally cars almost hit him, making him leap sideways with fright into the melting snow. He would stay there panting for a few minutes, then continue his aimless wandering.

Scarcely four days ago the tiny, nameless, unloved dog was still snuggled against his master – a kind, gentle man, who scratched his head and opened a tin when he was hungry. Sometimes, when he thought of that, Mambo would find the strength to raise his head and sniff the wind in case there might perhaps be some trace . . .

He passed by what was left of the snowdrift removed by the plough that morning. Water was still running from it on the roadway. Thinking it might give some temporary relief from his hunger and thirst, Mambo chewed a bit of snow, which had been sent flying through the country-side on the previous night by a wild wind, before piling up there.

It was in these compacted crystals that Mambo thought he could detect some trace of his lost master. The scent unwound along the ground, scarcely perceptible, like an invisible thread. Sometimes he lost it; sometimes he found it again. A desperate burst of energy sharpened his sense of smell. He buried his nose in the dead grass that protruded through the snow. He would stop suddenly, stretching his little body to see over the scrub, and try to make something out in the distance. He kept at it patiently, covering ten metres, stopping, starting off again, a wild hope pushing him on faster and faster.

Further away, a laurel-tree wood shivered in the wind, dominated from a great height by one lone cypress. The edge of the wood was some distance back from the road, and the rough outline of a path meandered towards it between fields green with autumn crops of wheat and rye. This was the path that attracted Mambo. He quivered with impatience before the abrupt black horizon of stiff trees, stuck in the wet humus like the pikes of an army rooted to the spot. Mambo searched for a way in through the closely planted forest edge. He scratched the ground, sniffed the turned earth, looking in all directions to try to get his bearings, whimpering, not knowing which way to turn.

Suddenly the daylight showed him a long, easy track opening out into the woods at the end of the path he had been following. He resolutely made for the opening.

The laurel branches knocked together above his head with a sound of clashing lances. Somewhere within the indescribable perfume of their leaves there lingered a smell that was still vague, but which wove itself more and more densely over the path of hard leaves where the dog was trotting.

In the shadows far ahead of him stood the solid bars of a rusty gate set in the middle of a high wall. Mambo was now advancing at the speed of a dog who recognised a friend approaching and hurries to catch up with him. He even began to wag his tail happily.

The track widened on each side of the wall. A stone cube, which had formerly been used as a seat, now came into view, padded with several seasons of dead leaves. Mambo stood on his hind legs, trying to reach the bars, but they were too high for him. He fell back on his tail.

Then, in a voice that did not seem to belong to him, forced from his small body, he let out a long, desolate howl. It was *mezza voce*, but travelled a great distance.

From a farm several kilometres away, a second dog began in a minor key. Two others answered him in New Montsalier. The repeated wave of sound struck the ears of old Médor, the best-fed basset hound in Banon, who joined the bass notes of his vocal cords to this chorus of dogs. The lament echoed around the laurel woods trembling in the wind, where Mambo, his nose pointing to the sky, gave voice to his haunting lament.

Sometimes fallow lands in this region contain desolate graves swept by the branches of a lone cypress, the last and only refuge of Protestants banished from cemeteries by the Church 400 years ago. They are mostly graves without stones or names, only remembered by ploughmen, who avoid them from one generation to the next, thus creating those strange diamond-shaped spaces where the heads of hemlock flourish.

Sometimes, though, they are real chapels surrounded by stone walls – the pride of those lords who rebelled against king and pope. Who did they belong to? The names on the vertical pediment and on the flagstones inside the tombs have been attacked with a sledgehammer. Devolution of inheritances to the State, sales of national assets, families dying out, have turned them into anonymous rural monuments, where the cypresses planted when the tombs were built now reach up to twenty metres into the sky.

It was in front of the iron gate of just such a tomb that Mambo was baying at the moon.

Roseline gave a few grunts then stopped in her tracks. Suddenly, with a sharp jerk, she pulled the lead from Alyre's hands, gave him the slip and ran off towards the edge of the wood.

"Good Lord! This is the limit! Just look at her! You'd think her back-side was on fire. Where on earth is she going? Roseline! Roseline!"

But all that could be seen of Roseline was her pink haunches bobbing up and down as she ran, and the lead flying behind her in the breeze. She was already heading into the undergrowth.

"Damn it, Roseline! I think you're about to get the first kick in the arse you've ever had in your whole life."

It was his turn to run up to the path, scattering the dead leaves as he went. He arrived at the iron gate of the tomb out of breath, without time to think. Roseline was sitting with her snout snuffling the dachs-hund's head raised to the moon. The dog's mouth was wide open and it was howling with all its strength.

"Good Lord, Roseline! It's the lost dog that everyone's been kicking around. What's he doing there?"

His jaw dropped. A strange idea had suddenly struck him; some-thing he'd been thinking about on and off since the beginning of autumn; since he'd had to chase after Roseline when she had bolted several times at the edge of this wood.

"Good Lord, Roseline! I knew it! That's it! Let's get out of here fast. That's what I couldn't manage to say. That's what I wanted to say."

He had already put the lead back on Roseline but she resisted him with all of her four legs and her considerable weight. It was useless pulling, she obstinately stayed sniffing the wretched dachshund baying at the moon.

They had been working together long enough for Alyre to under-stand all his sow's reactions.

"What! You want me to take him with me?" he exclaimed.

"Cro!" went Roseline.

"But what the hell will I do with him?"

"Cro!" went Roseline.

Alyre had no desire to argue the point. He felt as if he was choking, and just wanted to get out of there as quickly as possible. He bent down. The dog wanted to get away, but was too weak, and stumbled. Alyre grabbed him and slipped him between his jacket and chest. It was the only place where he could stop the dog from escaping. The dachshund shivered with misery, then just gave up the struggle and lay there.

"Come on, Roseline! Let's get out of here."

But Roseline kept up her passive resistance. Her snout was making a furrow in the dead leaves.

"What is it now?"

"Cro!" went Roseline.

She was standing the way she always did when she detected a truffle – stationary, snuffling, absolutely still. Alyre crouched down beside her.

"Oh! Good Lord! Roseline!"

With his free hand, Alyre had just taken hold of something in the dead leaves below the sow's head. He pulled and it kept on coming. It took him some seconds to identify it.

"Good Lord, Roseline! Do you know what it is? It's the kind of necklace that all those tramps wear. It's a scapular. Made of cypress wood beads. There's a sort of round notebook hanging on the end of it. Good Lord, Roseline! Run! Let's get out of here. I think you've uncovered some weird goings-on."

"That was it!" Alyre proclaimed in the gendarmes' van.

He balanced himself as well as he could on the heap of the three hippies the gendarmes had rounded up at Montsalier during the afternoon. They had to be carried to the van: they couldn't keep on their feet. If someone let go of them for any reason, they just collapsed in their sleeping bags. One was separate from the other two, who clung together in the same huge bag. Laviolette recognised them as the couple he had seen the other day making love behind the altar. They gave the impression that they were still caressing each other; that they couldn't do anything else; that they didn't want to do anything else. They had to be taken out of the church together, dragged off to the van and dumped on the floor like sacks of mail. Alyre's feet were resting on them.

"That's what I wanted to say," Alyre said again, "what I'll tell Francine tonight, and what I didn't dare say for fear of her laughing at me!

'Francine, do you think it's possible for people who have been dead for four hundred years to still smell?' "

He slapped his thighs. There, it was out at last, this very important thought that he had held back for three months. He repeated it to the gendarmes.

"Tell me, do you think it's possible?"

Night had fallen. There were no moon, nor stars in the sky other than the lights of Banon close by, those of Simiane down in the valley, and a few glimmers towards Carniol and La Rochegiron in the distance.

The laurel wood was surrounded by gendarmes and firemen, who would not allow anyone past. Reinforcements had been called in from Saint-Étienne, Forcalquier, plus refuse workers, a dump truck and two vans . . . just in case. They were all ready to get down to the job. The happy forensic lads from Criminal Records had just arrived back after another Marseilles–Banon car race, improving their record by another four minutes. All their equipment was unpacked and they were straining at the leash.

On the track with the dead leaves, a generator was throbbing. Floodlights on stands were being set up on long leads of electric cables. A few snowflakes could be seen floating in their beams.

Inspectors Guyot and Leprince had come back with the forensic men from Criminal Records. They had counted on going out that evening, and were not exactly pleased with this new complication.

Martel the mechanic's Land Rover bumped along the track, with another generator in tow.

You had to hold your nose and breathe through your mouth to keep going. That didn't stop some hardy locals from trying to slip into the woods and climb the wall of the tomb for a front seat. The gendarmes had just marched off two recidivists, threatening them with a kick up the backside if they appeared again. There were easily twenty people from Banon in the area, making prognostications and regretting they were not firemen. Slightly further away a small, animated group of drunken stragglers from the wedding party was recognisable by the strips of net floating on their cars and the white carnations attached to their rear-view mirrors. They could be seen hopping from one foot to the other in their best shoes, but would not have given up their vantage point for the world.

XVI

THE LOCAL CORRESPONDENT FROM *LE PROVENÇAL* HAD received a tip-off from a friend, and here he was with his Zeiss-Ikon around his neck ready for the first scoop of the day. He hadn't permission to be there, but that didn't matter. He was alone. He was the *only* journalist present. He had already phoned the paper to tell them to set aside three columns on page one. They wouldn't be sorry. It was already nine o'clock in the evening. Anything he could find out would be an exclusive story.

A black car, respectfully escorted, approached slowly from the end of the track, and stopped in front of the iron gate. The gendarme who had been guiding the driver opened the back door and saluted.

A slender young woman got out, blinking behind her glasses in the harsh glare of the lights. She would not have weighed very much. Her hair was neatly done, and she was not exactly beautiful, but not ugly either.

She held out her gloved hand to Laviolette and the chief, who stood to attention. She excused herself for having made them wait.

"The directions were not very good," she said. "My driver took the wrong turning." She gave a little laugh. "We drove right into a wayside chapel. It was quite an adventure."

Martel walked up to the gate. Chief Viaud had asked him to come as he used to be a locksmith before he owned the garage; it was a family tradition from father to son. The scene looked as if everyone was waiting for some president to emerge. The lock was the focal point of all the beams of white light, which eliminated the slightest shadow.

"You'll notice straight away," Viaud said, "that this enormous lock has recently been greased."

And indeed, there was a clearly visible ring around the keyhole.

"All to the good!" Martel whispered to the gendarme. "It'll make the job easier."

One of the nimble Criminal Records boys leaned over the rusty old lock and applied a kind of blotting paper around the hole, pressing it against the iron as hard as he could.

"What's that for?" Martel asked.

"To analyse the kind of lubricant that's been used."

"Oh, right."

The same process was applied to the hinges, which had also been greased. Following right behind, the second inspector photographed each one with a rapid series of flashes.

"Can I start?" Martel asked.

"Sure."

Martel had attached a ring of heavy keys to his belt. They were chosen from his large collection, just in case they might fit. "A Protestant tomb," he'd said to himself, "is no Yale lock. If a key still exists, it would have been one of my great-grandfathers who made it. I'll take this bunch of church keys and . . . let's see . . . yes! This big picklock. We'll see what we can do."

He bent over the box-shaped lock, looked through the hole and saw that it had no barrel. That was one difficulty eliminated . . . He inserted a good squirt of penetrating oil on to the mechanism. Then he searched around in the bunch of keys for a few minutes. He did some filing on one, pressed fairly hard as he turned it to the right, then to the left. He heard the noise of the bolt sliding. Once . . . twice . . . Then he concentrated his efforts on the knob of the slide, which gave him more trouble to shift than the lock itself.

"Can I push now?" he asked.

"Push but don't go any further," Laviolette said, "and move to the side."

Despite the grease on its hinges, the cemetery gate turned with a loud grating noise that set your teeth on edge.

Laviolette stood aside. The specialists moved the lights, switched on their flashes, and coordinated the details of their observations. Then they disappeared inside. Other floodlights were carried in after them and put in place. Finally Laviolette, the chief, two gendarmes and a clerk filed in through the opening.

All the men were talking very nasally, as they were holding their noses as tightly as possible. Standing with them was Madame Deputy Public Prosecutor, pressing a tiny handkerchief against her small nose. They were ready to come to her aid if need be, but there was nothing in her dainty person to indicate that she was going to faint. As someone experienced in such things, Laviolette had to admire her, for they were literally enveloped in the smell of death.

Once the gate was closed again, they began to hear the cypress sighing in the wind. The floodlights only showed up the grey base of the tree; the rest of its bushy height was lost in the black sky. The photoflashes sometimes lit up the trunk to a height of fifteen metres, but the crest swayed in the dark. A crop of thistles on the 200 square metres of enclosed land around the chapel poked their heads out of the shadows. Someone had walked through them, sometimes even savagely flattening them with a stick.

Armed with cameras, measuring tapes, powders, various instruments with dials that their colleagues called gadgets, the industrious inspectors from the Criminal Records Office crawled around this path.

"Prints?" asked Laviolette.

"Socks," was the reply.

"Shit!"

"Tsk, tsk . . . It's not a foregone conclusion . . . It all depends on the quality of the socks . . ."

110

"I bet you my pay against yours that they were bought at the Forcalquier market."

The procession regrouped in front of the tomb itself. Twenty lights searched its austere exterior, illuminating everything down to the joining of the stones, the smallest spot of lichen or damp. It was a dour-looking dry-stone chapel. The family name on the pediment had been hammered in such a way that 400 years later you could still feel the zealot's aggression. He had also tried to uproot the base on the sundial, but had only succeeded in twisting it.

"Can I try it now?" Martel asked.

The forensic inspectors, who had just examined the three marble steps and the door, stood back to let the artisan do his job.

This lock gave Martel a lot of bother, but he managed it without much noise or swearing. He gulped before asking,

"Will I open it?"

"Yes!" Laviolette said.

Two big rats squeaked in reply to the creaking of the warped door as it scraped over the marble. Playing leapfrog on the steps, they tried to escape by twice running around Madame Deputy Public Prosecutor's shoes. She showed not the slightest reaction, despite the fact that they had released a smell of human decay that would make the hardiest think again.

"Ugh!" groaned Martel, who hadn't said a word until then.

"Excuse us," the forensic men from the Criminal Records Office said as they passed in front of him. "In the police, you know, we rarely get to work on fresh corpses!"

Madame Deputy hid a smile behind her pretty handkerchief. The fingerprint guy was already crawling about down below in the beam of the spotlight, almost touching the corpses' feet with his forehead in his feverish hunt for clues.

It was a rich man's chapel; a chapel 7 x 4 metres, where pride, in its plainness, was no less evident than in Catholic splendour. Nothing. Just four walls. A roof so well put together that not a drop of water had got through in four centuries. A plain lead-light window with thick bars.

At the back was an inscription which, for some obscure reason, had escaped the attention of the zealot with the hammer. It was the only concession to sorrow: "When the even was come, Jesus saith unto them, 'Let us pass over unto the other side.'"

It was under this comforting invitation that the bodies of the five missing hippies had been placed. They were neatly laid out on the marble floor, with hands together like recumbent figures on a tomb. Had they been made of marble, they would have looked heraldic. Unfortunately they were made of flesh, and their body matter had spread around them in a halo on the paving stones, banishing pity.

In the lightning flashes of the cameras, the faces dissolving over the bones retained no more than vague outlines of what they once were. Only the matted hair kept its fullness and colour. The men's beards had grown.

Those rats must have been voles. They had not taken a great interest in the bodies, contenting themselves with gnawing the extremities.

"Have you finished?" Laviolette asked.

"Yes, as much as is humanly possible," the Criminal Records Office men replied.

"Did you measure the distance between the bodies?"

They turned towards him, looking surprised.

"No doubt. Besides, the photos . . ."

"Did you . . . search them?"

"Grosso modo . . . They were only wearing robes . . . Rings made of vegetable material; no wedding rings. Tomorrow at the morgue we'll take dental impressions, if that's possible, and collect everything they have on them. It'll be easier there . . ."

Laviolette was looking at the photos in his hand, trying to compare the happy young faces with the distorted forms of dissolving, flaccid flesh where, except in the more recent corpses, the only thing that stood out was the tip of the nasal cartilage. It was a difficult job matching them, but the Deputy Prosecutor joined him in working out this macabre jigsaw. She proved to be extremely competent, and Laviolette managed fairly quickly to classify the five missing persons in order.

"Are the hippies from Montsalier still here?" he asked.

"Yes. In the van."

"Go and fetch them."

"Fetch them! Carry them, more like!"

"What do you mean, 'carry them'?"

"Well, one's sound asleep, I think, and the other two are making love. Oh! Sorry, Ma'am!"

Chief Viaud had just realised that he was speaking in the presence of Madame Deputy Public Prosecutor.

"Not at all, not at all," she said. "Under the present circumstances, it seems to me to be a very appropriate thing to do . . ."

She took off her glasses and wiped them. The two men noticed that she had beautiful eyes.

She turned to the chief.

"Here you are. It's the list drawn up by the clerk. Keep on with your investigations, but as you have the files and addresses, it would be useful if you could inform the gendarmes in the relevant areas so that they can contact the families as quickly as possible . . . and get them to come here," she added. "Has the transfer of the bodies been arranged? Is there a morgue in Banon?"

"A rudimentary one," the chief said, "and, as things have turned out, remarkably small for the purpose."

The two of them talked quietly about urgent measures that needed to be taken.

Meanwhile, four exhausted gendarmes were lugging the three hippies in their sleeping bags like the corpse of Abbé Faria.* "Be careful not to kick them," the chief had warned them. Their feet were fairly itching in their shoes, all the same! But they had some satisfaction in dropping their bundles unceremoniously on the marble flagstones.

The vagrants did not react at first: one was still lost in his nirvana, and the other two in their mutual pleasuring, as if this new world they were in did not exist. At the level where they were breathing, however,

---

* A reference to Dumas' *The Count of Monte Cristo*. The old Abbé Faria is Edmond Dantès's companion in the Château d'If prison. When he dies and is sewn into a canvas shroud to be thrown into the sea, Dantès escapes by taking his place.

the smell of their former mates hit them full force. The world suddenly came into sharp focus: the ceiling, Laviolette, Madame Deputy Prosecutor, the inscription on the back wall. One was a little Italian with pointy features like d'Annunzio, a shaven face and head, graced only by a military moustache with long tapered ends, and the pigtail of a Chinese ready to be carried off into the great beyond. The other sleeping bag held a tall blond Dutchman with a beard and few teeth, and a hairy Dutchwoman with biceps like a stevedore, who must have weighed at least seventy kilos. They were talking in their own language about being woken up so abruptly. The Italian stood close to them for protection. Then, terror-stricken, they pointed to the bodies lined up on the ground.

"Constantin!"

"Chinchilla!"

"Patsy!"

"Ismaël!"

They swallowed hard, absolutely terrified.

"And the other one?" Laviolette asked.

"The other one?" the tall Dutchman said.

"Yes, the other one. The one in the middle. Isn't he a mate of yours?"

All three shook their heads, then turned away and went to the back wall, where they vomited copiously under Jesus' invitation. The sound of the three of them retching made a striking trio.

"Take advantage of the fact that they're still on their feet," Laviolette said. "Take them away, and while you're about it, show them the guy from the freezer. We still don't know who he is. They might be able to give us his name."

"Ma'am," he said, turning to the Deputy Prosecutor, "I think that's all we have to do here."

He was going out the gate when he saw a young blonde woman coming towards him. She stood out against the darkness because of all the bright light she reflected as she moved. Madame Deputy Prosecutor was less than thrilled by this vision.

"Why are they letting the public in?" she said. "Who is she? What's she doing here?"

"Unfortunately, we suspect that her brother may be one of the victims," Viaud said. "That's her," he whispered to Laviolette, "the one I was telling you about. Claire Piochet."

He went over to her, as much out of deference to the Deputy Prosecutor, who didn't want any other woman but herself near the body, as to show his concern for the poor girl at a loss and alone. He said something to her softly, and gently led her away.

"Just a moment," Laviolette said.

He turned to Viaud.

"I've told her it's likely that . . ." the chief said.

The girl was crying, but without sound or movement. The tears seemed to well up in her big eyes in spite of herself.

"My brother . . ?" she whispered.

"We can't say for certain" Laviolette replied. "You'll know tomorrow. For the time being, you should get some rest."

"I want to look!"

Laviolette shook his head.

"It's not possible at the moment. We'll call you in tomorrow."

He watched her as she left, supported by Viaud, who was obviously being extremely obliging.

"By Jove!" Laviolette murmured to himself. "That girl will always find someone to look after her . . ."

"Did you notice her coat?" added the Deputy Prosecutor, who had overheard him. "It's imported from Scotland. There would only be about a hundred coats like that in France. They're incredibly dear . . ."

"She does seem to be dreadfully upset," Laviolette said.

"Yes, dreadfully . . ." the Deputy said, expressing some doubt.

She watched Claire's departing figure with great attention.

Laviolette had the impression that Madame Deputy Prosecutor did not look kindly at any possible rivals. And it was true that she herself was not without charm.

"I know what you're thinking," she said, "being the man you are. But it's not that at all. I was just asking myself an absurd question. I was wondering if one could be dreadfully upset and still sway one's hips like that? What do you think?" she asked, suddenly turning to Laviolette.

He shook his head.

"Don't expect me to give you an answer to such a serious question," he replied, "without due consideration . . ."

The various services involved needed another two hours to complete the investigation. The gendarmes went back to the station and began writing, telephoning, sending messages, answering questions. In the presence of Laviolette, they questioned Alyre, Georgette, the kitchen hand and the hotel owner, all of whom had to make sworn statements.

Metre by metre, the forensic specialists from Criminal Records examined the whole surface area of the cemetery among the thistles, which pricked their legs badly. They accompanied the corpses to the hospital in relays, so that there was always someone present. The bodies could not be shown to their families naked, but it was also important to keep a check on their clothes – such as they were – the amulets and rings, which had to be analysed.

The forensic pathologist arrived at 4.00 a.m. and waited outside the home of his local colleague, who had gone to give a morphine injection for a kidney-stone attack to the butcher in Revest-des-Brousses.

"Do you have to come at this hour?" Dr Lusel said, when his colleague introduced himself.

"'No let-up!', as they say in the police manual," he replied with a smile on his face.

The hospital management were at a loss to know where to put all the bodies, especially as the two sixteen-year-olds who were responsible for the accident on Saturday night had not yet been claimed by their families.

At the old men's home next door, a kind of happy expectation lightened the dodderers' coughing spells. They would certainly have something to talk about in the morning.

*

Without a word, Rosemonde, who was still up, pushed a bowl of soup and a cup of coffee that would waken the dead towards Laviolette slumped in a chair.

"No let-up!" Laviolette said.

He had scarcely swallowed four spoonfuls of soup before he fell asleep on the walnut table, his head resting on his arms.

Day broke over Banon.

XVII

"FORENSIC! I KNOCKED BUT YOU DIDN'T HEAR ME . . ."

It was eleven o'clock on Monday morning. A mournful wind was blowing over Banon. From under the yellow eiderdown, Laviolette watched his breakfast being carried in Rosemonde's plump hands.

"Do you think you could manage to eat something?" she said.

"I'll try."

She went out, standing aside for the forensic pathologist who was showing all his false teeth in a broad smile. Dr Grégoire Rabinovitch, State-accredited doctor and right-hand man at the Public Prosecutor's Office, had greedy lips and a swarthy complexion. He was completely bald with a pitted head caused by various accidents both military and automobile. The young inspectors called him "Angle Head". It had facets like a diamond, but inside, the brain was quite intact. Woken at 2.00 a.m., in Banon by 4.00, he had been working since then with the local doctor on decomposed bodies, but you'd never know it to look at him.

"Thank you," he said, "for your generous concern! My word! Six at one blow!"

He looked at the tray, the blue cup and coffee pot, the plate holding slices of toast with little birds on them.

"Oh happy man," the doctor exclaimed, "to be breakfasting on two thrush on canapés!"

"They're *chachas!*"* growled Laviolette, who liked them very hot, very brown and very crisp, just the way they were presented to him on the tray.

"Can I talk without ruining your appetite?"

"No need to beat about the bush," said Laviolette.

"Well then, a priori and despite the state they were in, I can already tell you that your bodies from the tomb, plus the fresh one from the freezer – which was already about two days old . . . Well, I can already tell you that they had all been hung up by the feet and drained of their blood!"

"What do you mean? Drained of their blood?"

"Like pigs! The blade of a knife has been slowly turned in the carotid artery to get a good blood flow."

"Do you mean . . . that they were bled . . . alive?"

"More or less. I have bottles of the organs in the boot of my car. We won't get anything from at least three – the oldest of them – but analysis of the most recent will give some interesting data. In all probability they were dead drunk or drugged when whoever it was began to bleed them."

"That's why," Laviolette said to himself, "'whoever it was' needed someone unremarkable, all-purpose, not much to look at . . . This kind of thing only happens to me. The others always get nice big cases of gangsters or pimps with their bellies full of holes. And me? I get lumbered with these lunatics! Bled like pigs! I ask you!

"When will we have the results of these tests?" he asked.

"I'm going to deliver the specimens right away," Rabinovitch said. "For the simple tests: tomorrow morning. For the more complex procedures, in . . . let's say, four or five days."

"You mean for Christmas!" Laviolette said grimly.

"Yes, that's it," Rabinovitch said as he was leaving. "For Christmas! For Christmas!" he repeated, rubbing his hands.

*

* Male thrush, which are bigger and more expensive than the normal variety.

The market was in full swing when he went down. The agents set up only twice a year in Banon, on the Mondays before and after Christmas. For the rest of the year, the harvest had to be taken to them in Forcalquier. The usual smell of the house was intensified by a fresh, new one that morning. The smell of truffles that came up the stairs to meet Laviolette was so strong it seemed almost solid.

Those semi-mythical characters, the truffle agents, officiated each at his own table in the shade. One of them, quite tall and quite old, wore a monocle and used to say he kept in shape for the ladies by eating two or three truffles cooked in the ashes every morning. He stored his purchases in a huge wicker basket, placing them inside with great care. The other one, who was more the buccaneer type, had a golden smile. The locals stood cowering before his two rows of gold teeth, like Little Red Riding Hood before the wolf in Grandma's clothing. They filed past apprehensively with their little bag or basket, not saying a word; above all those – and there were a lot of them – who had never owned a single truffle tree in their lives, yet were at all the markets. You could recognise them by their sharp faces, looking more wary than most of the genuine owners. They usually sandwiched themselves between one or two large producers, carrying their half, or sometimes full, kilo in a clear plastic bag. The agent with the gold teeth piled everything up together and threw them down into big opaque bags used for carrying bread. Later in the day, he would hoist the bags unceremoniously on to his shoulder to carry them to the car. When he had to pay – and it was as seldom and little as possible – he would bring out a fat, rough wallet which refused to slide easily out of his pocket. He was not liked. He swindled you. But he did take everything, all mixed up together: large and small, ripe and green, while the other one, the one with the monocle, was always finding fault. He would sometimes raise a suspicious finger and flick a tiny piece off a fine truffle, and if he found it not very ripe, he would quickly lower the price by thirty to forty francs a kilo.

Laviolette recognised everyone in the crowd at the hotel, especially the well-dressed gentlemen at the counter, some with cameras around their necks, who were eagerly watching for him as for the Messiah. They advanced towards him as soon as he appeared.

Times had changed. In the old days there would have been thirty of them helping Rosemonde's business along. Now they drank nothing but fruit juice and, apart from the three correspondents from the regional dailies, the French and foreign press had only three representatives from international agencies. Tomorrow their reworked and embellished drafts would be sold to the dailies and weeklies in the same form, but cut and pasted to shorten or lengthen the text. You could expect the truth to be based on some vague memories of something they had read.

"Gentlemen," Laviolette said, "I would appreciate it if you would come and see me tonight at the police station. I'll fill you in then. For the moment, I've work to do."

He went to mingle with the truffle hunters, who had the fresh smell of the hills about them. He felt sure that someone in that cautious crowd knew something vital, something he would not tell anyone. Laviolette believed in thought osmosis. If one of those men harboured a thought, an idea or an obsession, moving amongst them would perhaps allow him to absorb it, to more or less become aware of it.

"Let the *Uillaoude* through!" someone shouted.

Everyone moved back courteously and perhaps with a hint of fear to let the gnarled old woman pass. She scarcely reached up to the men's waist in height, but bent over as she was, she and her cane occupied a space measuring a full cubic metre. She looked up at you from below with narrow, piggy eyes that made your blood run cold. Her head nodded with every step that took her rapidly towards the agent with the gold teeth. Nobody laughed. The *Uillaoude* had thrown her little bag of truffles on to the dish of the steelyard scales.

"Bring the beam closer, so that I can see it," she said in a shrill voice. "You always bring scales with a beam that's so worn you can't see the notches. I know you! What! Is that all!"

"I'm giving you good measure, *Uillaoude*."

And indeed, he was rounding up her 980 grams to a kilo and paying her 120 francs, which was what he paid for the best quality. You don't mess around with the *Uillaoude*. She admitted that in the past she had cast a few spells "to give a helping hand" here and there.

"But now," she said, "what with the 'tautomobile', the telly, rockets and all that, there's no call for it any more! I've retired from business."

When she said it, the word business had a sinister meaning.

"Oh!" she added casually. "It'll come back! It'll come back!"

"The *Uillaoude*," Laviolette said to Rosemonde, the first time he saw the old woman. "*Uillaou* in Provençal means lightning . . . The *Uillaoude* must be 'the woman as fast as lightning', don't you think? That could well be because of the way she rushes everywhere?"

"No, that's not it," Rosemonde replied. "She was struck by lightning in the storm of 1924, which killed two people. It twisted her up like a corkscrew. That's why she's called the *Uillaoude*."

On this particular day she was grumbling in front of the agent about the 320 francs she had just received.

"Well! I should have gone to Apt like my nephew. I don't know how he manages it. He had about ten kilos, the lucky thing."

"So, why couldn't he have sold them to me?" the agent said, showing his annoyance. "Does he think he'll get more at Apt?"

"I'm only repeating what he told me: 'I'm going to Apt. I get a better deal.'"

She turned round and went off at the distinctive speed which the lightning charge had given her long ago. The men jumped back to let her pass, even those who seemed too deep in an amusing conversation to take notice. One of them actually opened the door politely for her, so that she would be outside all the sooner.

Haute Provence had not gone out of its way to welcome the victims' families. Under a lowering sky, town council workers were getting outsiders' cars moved from the square, as they were occupying the place where the decorative Christmas trees were to be put. The victims' families were almost apologising for the fact that their children had been killed so near Christmas. And the whole demeanour of the council workers more or less suggested that it was true, that it was indeed a nuisance, and that they had just wasted a full hour searching at the police station for the owners of the five big cars in the square.

The families went to the police station, hanging their heads. The two offices were full of people, while gendarmes were busy copying identity cards. All these poor souls had been informed by the police very early in the morning. They had rushed into planes and cars, arriving freezing cold, exhausted, disorientated and in despair. They claimed their son, or daughter or niece. They wanted to see the body. The right words were said to calm them. The two inspectors and the gendarmes held their grief in check, getting them to give details, questioning them sympathetically. The clicking of keyboards kept a distance between them and the tragedy, deadening the sound of tears and mothers' cries.

The bodies had been laid out as neatly as possible in deal coffins made by the local carpenter, but no-one was in a hurry to take all these people to see them. The chief quietly let Laviolette know the identity of the victims' parents. There was Mr Spirageorgevich, the accountant, dressed like an English gentleman complete with umbrella, and his extremely large, bespectacled wife stoically gnawing at her handkerchief; Mr Ben Amozil, the merchant, whose son had become a plumber to spite him, a tall Semite sitting with his continually shaking head in his hands. He was alone. "Divorced – in his favour," Viaud explained. A fat Spaniard from Irun was introduced to Laviolette as the uncle of the missing Incarnacion Chinchilla. He looked more like a widower than an uncle. They had to wait for the plane from London to Marignane, where two inspectors went to meet Patricia McKetterick's mother. As for the last body – the one in the freezer – he did not fit any missing persons' enquiries from the families. He had no papers. The search at Montsalier had provided no clues. The interrogation of his companions had not revealed anything about him, or the other bodies for that matter. The living hippies had recovered quickly, i.e. they had once again refused to talk. They had made just one introductory statement, duly noted by the Deputy Prosecutor's scribe, which could be summed up as follows: that they didn't care whether they lived or died and that, morally speaking, they spat in the faces of all cops. That's what they wanted to say. And they had a last comment to add: that murderers are the direct result of the capitalist State which hides them away, and are consequently as much victims as the people they killed. Right. They could not be held against their will, especially as they were almost as smelly as their dead companions.

The families were taken to the hospital in the van for the official identification of the bodies. They did so with the greatest restraint possible, except for the Spaniard from Irun. He wanted to throw himself on the body of what had been his niece, which had been patched up with great difficulty, and clasp her in his arms. While three gendarmes forcibly restrained him, he poured out words of love punctuated with kisses to the poor lifeless creature who was there precisely because she wanted to escape from him.

Viaud supported Claire at the coffin of her brother, whom she officially identified, as she had wanted to do the previous night at the mausoleum. The others could not reply immediately to the policeman's question. They sometimes found it hard to connect what had happened with the strong young man with such a wholesome upbringing, the brilliant student in Political Science, or the lovely, sensuous girl they had known.

By four o'clock, everything was wrapped up. The parents were free to make their arrangements for taking the children who had escaped from them back to the family crypt. Claire was dry-eyed now. She seemed hard, determined.

"Are you leaving?" Laviolette asked.

"No, I'm staying. He doesn't need me any more. My uncles will take charge of the funeral. I'm staying. I'll find the murderer. I'll kill him! I swear to you, I'll kill him!"

"Come now!" Laviolette said. "You surely don't want to go to prison?"

She looked at him scornfully.

"My brother was right wanting to get away from a society like this."

Now that they had real bodies and not just vague missing persons, the police network brought out its big guns. The gendarmes circulated descriptions; the inspectors interviewed everyone in Banon, showing them photos.

"Have you seen this man or this girl with anyone? Where? When? What did the person he or she spoke to look like? Do you recognise this photo? Did this person ever speak to you? What was said?"

There were sixty basic questions, which should add some information to the case file. It was something to work on while waiting for more conclusive evidence.

At seven o'clock Laviolette and the chief, sitting opposite each another in the office, were mulling over the three questions that remained unanswered: why hippies; why hung up by the feet; why bled white?

"When we find the right answer to these three questions," Laviolette said, "we'll have the murderer. But there's something else that puzzles me: how did the murderer get a key to the tomb? Did he make it? Did he inherit it? Had it been left in trust to his forebears?"

"Whatever the answer, that key is central to the problem," the chief said. "Whether he's a descendant, a trustee, or he made it himself, the owner of that key is someone from this area."

"Not necessarily from Banon itself," Laviolette said, "but certainly from around here. It's risky carrying a body in some sort of vehicle over a very long distance. What's more, there are certainly several people who *know* who owns the key."

"All that needs to be done now," Viaud said as he drew a red circle around Banon on the ordnance map, "is to make tighter and tighter circles around the murderer."

"Why would someone from the region go and kill tramps," Laviolette said thoughtfully, "and in such a horrible way?"

"A madman?" suggested the chief.

"You don't believe that. Nor do I. But that's the angle we'll present to the journalists."

He gazed at the photo enlargement of the five bodies lined up on the marble floor of the Protestant tomb. He couldn't take his eyes off it. The whole group had been measured with a tape that the Criminal Records boys had rolled out across the floor above the heads of the victims. It lessened the horror of the picture by giving it an archeological touch.

"It's strange . . ." Laviolette said.

Viaud came around and looked over his shoulder.

"Look," Laviolette said, "the bodies are laid out in – pardon the expression – chronological order. The first, Constantin Spirageorgevich, is sixty centimetres from the back wall; the second, Incarnacion Chinchilla, a metre away from Constantin. There's the same one-metre space between Ismaël Ben Amozil and Patricia McKetterick. So why is the body of Jeremy Piochet, the most recent of them, put between the two girls, instead of after Ismaël, since there was enough space for him? Why was he slotted in between?"

"Why, you're right. But there's a whole heap of disconcerting things in this case. One more, or one less . . . I have an explanation!" he exclaimed suddenly. "Jeremy Piochet was in love with one of the girls, the murderer knew it, and in an act of some sort of posthumous piety . . ."

Laviolette turned his heavy gaze on the chief, who was a man of thirty, with a fresh, pink complexion, a wife and a baby. He saw the world in the idyllic light of his very normal home life.

"You should tell your appealing explanation to the journalists. They'd never stop playing with that chewing-gum."

Viaud smiled.

"Any human explanation is plausible," he said. "But of course we won't pass on our observations to the Press. Shall I call them in?"

"Do we have a choice . . . ?" sighed Laviolette.

XVIII

SNOW WHISTLED THROUGH THE NEEDLES OF THE FIR TREES that had been brought in to decorate the town square for Christmas. The festive coloured lights and bunting were now waving in the fierce wind. It was the same kind of weather we'd had on the previous Saturday night.

Throughout the evening, hearses had been nosing their way around those trees, asking anyone who was passing or watching how to get to the hospital so that they could take delivery of the bodies. Each family waited to follow and arrange a suitable wake at last for what had, in spite of everything, been the hope of their lives.

Partly because of the weather, this funeral cortège did not attract the attention of the population of Banon. At nine o'clock, when Laviolette came back from the police station, there were few people still outdoors. Cosily settled in front of the TV, they were all engrossed in various forms of reassuring consolation as they watched the soothing women announcers on the screen.

Rosemonde looked around her empty room.

"I think," she said, "that there will be just the two of us once again . . . With weather like this . . . Shall I serve your soup?"

She was walking out to prepare it for him, but stopped and came back.

"By the way," she said, "your friend Brèdes telephoned an hour ago."

"The marquis? What did he want?"

"He wanted you to call him back as soon as possible."

Laviolette went to the phone and dialled the number.

"Is that you, Laviolette?"

"Hello Brèdes. Are you inviting me to spend Christmas Eve with you?"

"I thought of it, but that's not why I called you. I called because I remembered something. I say, what an incredible story! Bled white? Are you sure?"

"How did you know that?" Laviolette asked.

"Oh, it's quite simple. My farmer's daughter is a wards maid at the hospital. She was cleaning the wash basins when the forensic pathologist and the local doctor came in for a piss. They were talking about their work. 'Bled white! Like pigs!' She repeated it to her mother. Since then they haven't stopped scaring each other with the story."

"Be careful!" Rosemonde called out from the kitchen. "If it's confidential, there are interferences on the line. When it snows in Banon, with all those relay antennas you can hear everything from everywhere."

She was shouting to make herself heard over the sizzling of the croutons she was frying with a drizzle of vinegar.

"What's Rosemonde saying there?" Brèdes asked.

"She asked me to say hello from her!"

"Good. Give her my love. Now tell me . . . I've had a really mad idea . . . really bizarre! You remember me telling you the other day about a book of mine that disappeared. Well, I remember what I was reading to amuse my guests, and . . ."

"Don't say another word!" Laviolette said, cutting him off in mid-sentence.

"But . . ."

"Not another word!"

Laviolette had thirty years experience of watching and waiting, and that took the place of radar, sonar or computer . . . For him Banon was a palpable presence in the howling of the storm. He had the impression

128

that hundreds of receivers had been lifted and a murderer was listening with bated breath at each of them.

"Walls have ears?" Brèdes asked.

"Walls are not the only things. Just stay where you are. You're at home, aren't you?"

"Warm and cosy in my library."

"Good. Make yourself comfortable and wait for me. I'm coming."

"You're coming here? In this weather?"

"Don't worry. I have chains. I'm coming, I tell you!"

"Not before you've had a plate of soup," Rosemonde said.

"Oh no! I can't."

"But it's cream of sorrel with grated truffle."

"My dear Rosemonde. You'll have to get used to it. That's a cop's life for you. No let-up!"

He was already out the door, swathed up to his eyes in his muffler like an Arab, his hat pulled down over his ears, and his heavy overcoat tightly buttoned. Even so, the storm whipped into him as if he had nothing on. The apple-green Vedette was hidden under the stark plane trees. But the tank-like Mercedes was missing. Where could the beautiful Claire be in such weather? Was she looking for the murderer?

It was already a very nasty night. A geyser of snow was blowing up from Les Aires gate, which we take as a sign that the elements are about to descend on us with a vengeance. Laviolette got behind the wheel. "You should have rolled yourself a cigarette while there was still time," he said to himself. "Before you knew! There'll be no let-up now!"

While he was driving down towards Dauban, as wads of snow hit his windscreen like big, soft paws, he repeated the basic police principles: "A statement should be taken down as soon as possible. If at all possible, on the spot, before the witness's immediate impression begins to fade . . ."

The storm was travelling towards Val Martine, towards the fossil-rich hills of Revest-des-Brousses. It swept up the Dauban valley like a rising wave before breaking against the Vachères spur, where the Gordes chestnut groves moaned in protest. There were thick black clouds, originally part of the major depression centred over Scandinavia, which the wind blew on to us in jagged bands. Sometimes the Great Bear could be seen lying above the Lure mountains through holes in the low sky, at other times it was Orion's Belt. Then everything suddenly closed up again and the banks of snow spread along the ground.

Laviolette bumped along with his purring eight cylinders, the chains on his wheels leaving a trail behind him. But thanks to them, he managed the icy hillside road to Saint-Laurent without incident. The superintendent's thoughts were far from cheerful.

"The murderer learned that the bodies had been discovered at the same time as me and the rest of Banon. He knows we know everything about them from the autopsy. Since then he's been searching for the detail or the witness that could lead us to him. He's at least as intelligent as me, and Brèdes. Brèdes has a theory that may be wrong or may be right. I'm still trying to work things out, but the murderer *knows* whether Brèdes' idea threatens him or not. Even if he didn't know about the first call to Rosemonde through the leaky telephone system in Banon, he's had the whole day to figure out that Brèdes was going to call me. Therefore . . ."

He could make out the lights of Brèdes' farmhouses beyond the pond in the Aubenas valley about 300 metres away. He immediately turned off on to the dirt road past the four huge cedars whose branches were blown out like sails. The gale moaned deep within them, as though it would never stop.

Beyond this curtain of trees, the Vedette's headlights lit up the sparse lawn with its rusty seats that no-one had sat on since the death of the old marquis ten years before. Brèdes had had the good idea of brightly lighting the covered porch that went along the outside of the manor house. Ghostly sheets of snow were torn into shreds as they hit the four rows of Roman tiles on the edge of the roof.

Laviolette parked close to the worn steps leading up to the porch. He shut the car door and put his foot on the first step. Then all the lights went out.

"Shit!"

He couldn't even see the toe of his shoes, or the side mirrors of the Vedette, or the small lights of the distant farm under a cloud-burst. He was sure to come a cropper if he went back to the car, although it was scarcely six metres away.

"Brèdes!" he called as loudly as he could. "Give me some light!"

The only reply he received came from the cedars breasting the wind like the bow of a ship.

"Brèdes!"

As his calls remained unanswered, he began to fear the worst. He regretted having come on his own. The smell of a hot engine, not from his car, lingered in the air at ground level. He groped his way towards the Vedette with his arms out in front of him. If he missed it, even by as little as fifty centimetres, he would go round in circles in the dark, which had turned the smiling countryside into a black wilderness.

Everything was in the glove box: his lighter, his tobacco pouch and an old torch. He hoped to heaven that it was still working. He suddenly came in contact with the Vedette – unfortunately it was his knee against the bumper bar.

"Shit!" he moaned.

He turned on the interior light in the car, found the torch and switched it on. It gave out a faint yellow beam that showed not more than two stone steps in front of him.

"Brèdes!"

The door to the long corridor was wide open and the snow was blowing in unchecked. Laviolette went in with it. Smoke from a fireplace disturbed by the draught floated in the air. But it carried traces of another smell.

"Brèdes!"

Just as he was calling out, his torch suddenly gave out. However, he then noticed a diffuse light on the left, coming from the room where he had had lunch the other day with his friend. That door was also wide open. He started to rush towards it, but there was a bench in his way. In the time it took to grab his knee and shout, "Bloody hell!', he was in front of the fire where his friend lay flat on his face beside the lectern. Laviolette saw that his hands were trying to clutch at something. Then he heard a curious sound like the glug of liquid pouring out of a bottle. It was coming from the body on the floor.

He turned quickly. In the firelight, the sight of the blood welling up from the slit carotid artery hit him like something out of a nightmare. Brèdes' eyes were open. Laviolette felt his neck for a second or two. His thumb felt for the hole in the artery – it was thirty years since he'd done this – sank deep into it, and turned. At the same time he put his free arm under his friend's neck to support him.

As he was performing these two precise actions, he was conscious of a slithering movement in the room. Someone was watching; someone was calculating. In the dying flashes of light that still came from a few embers in the hearth, a dark mass was suddenly outlined in the low doorway to the library. It slowly became more distinct on the other side of the corridor.

It was a solid shape, with no neck, no shoulders, no head, covered to the waist by black netting with small dots like a widow's veil. Laviolette knew that his gaze was crossing the murderer's behind the veil. There was a sigh of suppressed disappointment, and the apparition disappeared. Then came the sound of strange steps along the corridor; a dancing step moving swiftly, not at all inhibited by the darkness.

Laviolette had time to realise how powerless he was. If he took his thumb out of the artery, unblocking the carotid, the four and a half litres of blood his friend still had in him would gush out in two minutes, in 120 heartbeats. When the wind dropped a little, he could hear a recalcitrant engine that was having trouble starting. There were some clumsy manoeuvres, then the car finally drove away. Thirty seconds, forty seconds . . . By the light of the fire, he could see the second-hand of his watch relentlessly jerking forward.

"Can you hear me?" he said.

He looked directly into his friend's eyes with their already resigned expression. Brèdes blinked.

"Who?" Laviolette asked. "You know! Who? Make any kind of sign! A blink for a letter of the alphabet."

It began very slowly. The thought struck Laviolette that circulation in the brain had already been interrupted, and that the capillaries and blood vessels around the open artery would not have time to revive and make up for the loss. Sixty seconds. In this position, with the weight of the body, he could never drag himself to the telephone on the desk. He was stuck where he was, helpless to do anything; in as desperate a situation with the limp body of his friend as he would have been trying to hold a dying man up against a partition at 4000 metres altitude.

He counted the blinks. At letter F, Brèdes lost consciousness.

Then, inch by inch and panting with the effort, Laviolette began trying to get hold of his friend with one arm, the other one being useless as it had to compress the artery. He dragged himself along on his knees from one flagstone to the next, with his friend beneath him, begging his pardon all the while as he went. He had to give up when he got to the closed door to the office. He was there, painfully bent double, which meant that the door handle was out of reach. He searched for it, feeling his way with one hand. At last he found it. The slow crawl began again in the dim, flickering light from the library fire. The telephone was on a side-table, a metre and a half from the ground. Hindered by his overcoat, Laviolette had to lift his friend's weight with one arm for the length of the table, so that he could straighten up a little and grab the phone. And all the while the phosphorescent dial of his watch with its skipping second-hand was there practically beneath his nose. He jammed his knees under Brèdes' armpits. He had collapsed like a puppet. Laviolette picked up the receiver. Feeling for the dial like a blind man, with shaking hand he rang the police station.

When Viaud and three of his men with their powerful lights rushed out of the van, Laviolette hardly had the strength to call out, "Over here!"

They found him bent over, looking haggard, with his thumb still in his friend's carotid artery. His mouth was open and he was panting like an old man having a heart attack. Viaud leaned over Brèdes' body.

"He's dead!" he declared.

He looked at Laviolette who wasn't listening to him, stubbornly keeping his thumb buried in the hole.

"He can't be!" he groaned. "I did everything I could. I did everything I could. No-one could have done more."

He was a tough man, but heavy tears were running down his cheeks.

Viaud took him by the arm to make him let go. There was a sound like an unblocked pipe. Thick blood flowed over Laviolette's hand, covering it like a glove in a horror film.

XIX

"THE BOOK THAT WAS ON THE LECTERN, THE ONE YOU
wanted to burn because you thought it was heretical. Do you remember?
What was it called?"

The farmer's wife, stiff-backed and dressed entirely in black, looked
Laviolette full in the face. Her daughter, who had heard the doctors in
the hospital, was supporting her with all the strength of her healthy
young woman's body. Like most of the peasants around here at this
time of the year, the husband was on his land digging for truffles.

"I knew it!" the farmer's wife said. "I knew he should have burned
it. He laughed when I spoke to him about it. God help him!"

It was the cry of a mountain woman overcome by misfortune. You
felt that she had loved Brèdes more than her own family, like an
institution.

"Maman!" the daughter said gently, "They've no time to waste. Tell
them the name of the book."

"*Le Grand Albert*," she whispered.

Laviolette tried to remember what that title reminded him of. Yes
. . . That was it! Albert the Great, the seventeenth-century alchemist.
His name had been exploited and several dozen treatises on witchcraft
in all the languages of Europe had been attributed to him. What was

this one hiding? Who had it? How could he locate an identical copy to find a clue which would help solve the problem?

Viaud and his two gendarmes had already called it a day. Their clerk had finished taking the woman's statement. Neither she, her husband nor her daughter, had heard a thing. The dogs hadn't even barked. It must be said, of course, that there were more than 300 metres between the farm and the manor.

Up in the old silkworm house, the forensic boys from Criminal Records and the inspectors were searching the building for the book or any other clue.

Laviolette was reluctant to call out the vast police and criminal investigation network to hunt for another edition of the book in a library somewhere. And besides . . . how could you be sure that it was the same? How could you convince an extraordinary number of sceptics, who would be reluctant to get mixed up in anything like this, for fear of being made a laughing-stock? A treatise on witchcraft? You must be joking! The National Library, the Mazarine Library . . . All the old collections from all over France to search, all their catalogues, which were often incomplete . . . Too bad! It had to be done! He gave Viaud a notice to be communicated to police stations and gendarmerie posts everywhere.

He telephoned his superiors from the farmhouse to justify his search as well as he could. There was no other clue apart from this tenuous lead and the very vague report of a car with chains in the square at Banon on the night of the accident.

It was when he went out into the early morning air that the memory of his dead friend really hit him. He screwed up his cigarette paper and threw it away without filling it.

"It's just too bloody stupid!" he said to himself. "To have been through so much! Risked so much! Only to have death catch up with you in Vachères of all places! Amid that peace and quiet . . . and by a butcher! If only I'd paid more attention!"

He tried to think back to their last meeting. In his mind, he went over the whole conversation about the book, how it was found in the lectern and how it disappeared. Everything they said . . . But it's difficult to remember a rambling conversation on a relaxed afternoon, with nothing more pressing to do than gently warm a balloon of good brandy in your palms.

He put out a hand to stop Viaud, who was leaving to send out his instructions.

"Wait!" he exclaimed. "I'm trying to put things together. I'm sorry. Just thinking about it won't do any more. I have to find my ideas by talking out loud, like a peasant. Now, it's more or less a quotation from Stendhal . . . Wait! He said to me . . . He was talking about Bébé Fabre, someone we both knew well when we were kids . . . His father – Brèdes' that is – had found the book in a lectern he bought from Bébé . . . Just a moment . . . In 1930 . . . In 1930, he was saying . . ."

His hand suddenly tightened on the chief's sleeve.

"That's it! I've got it! 'I have another!' That's what Bébé Fabre said to Brèdes' father, who offered to give the book back to him. I have another! I have another!"

"More than fifty years ago!" Viaud said, looking very disappointed.

"Fifty years!" Laviolette replied. "What's fifty years for a book? We're the ones who disappear and are replaced. You can't imagine how many things stay the same in fifty years. Chief, take me to Manosque. In the van."

"Superintendent, with all due respect, you've had it."

"You don't owe me any respect. I'm a stupid old bastard. I let my friend get killed because my brain's not what it was. Take me to Manosque of your own free will, if you don't want me to order you to do it. I'll sleep in the van, on the stretcher. And here you are. Take my tobacco pouch . . . and my rice papers. Can you roll your own?"

Viaud smiled.

"You learn almost everything being a gendarme."

"Well, then, roll me one, will you? I'm bushed . . . I'll lick the edge of the paper when you've finished."

He lay down on the stretcher in the van and gave two puffs. Viaud mercifully took the cigarette out of his mouth before it fell on his tie.

Laviolette fell asleep in the middle of the order he was forever repeating. "No let-up! No delay . . ."

Held up by the Highways Department trucks clearing snowdrifts off the roads, they arrived in Manosque at about ten o'clock. There were so many cars in town and such anarchy on the narrow streets that the police van could not get through.

They woke Laviolette, who was sleeping with his mouth open, making a noise like an old grindstone. He was wide awake in an instant, looking around to get his bearings. He led the gendarmes up towards Aubette, by Le Chacundier corner. On the way, he pointed triumphantly to a sort of red brick rabbit hutch at the bottom of Rue Danton. It had a latched door, jagged and worn at the base.

"There you are! Nearly fifty years. You see! When I was sent here on holidays at my grandmother's place, I would meet a little girl of ten, adorably precocious, who would try as hard as she could to bring my little dick to life. Poor thing, I was only six. It was in there. In that hut. On a big stone that must still be there. She sat on it and made me stand in front of her. And look! The door is just the same. It hasn't changed a bit. It's just as worm-eaten, and the bricks are just as worn. I recognise the crack that looks like an aubergine. Nearly fifty years! You see how little difference fifty years can make?"

But an abbey is not a brick rabbit hutch . . .

One day a mayor had noticed some aesthete go into raptures over the unusual quadruple rows of Roman tiles under the roof of the old convent, which Bébé Fabre had used for half a century to store all his jumble of antiques. Mayors are not too happy about people admiring what they themselves don't understand. This one was particularly touchy on the subject. Henceforth he had his eye on that masterpiece, and promised himself that at the first opportunity . . .

Laviolette felt quite lost. He looked about him for some trace of his childhood in the terrace with its mosaic tiles, packed full of big cars. He noticed an old man sitting on a bench, who kept drawing and rubbing out shapes in the dust with his cane.

"Wasn't there a convent here before?"

"There certainly was! A bit of it's still there."

He pointed to big walls that had been done over with ochre roughcast. They seemed to bulge out a little.

"And the tree . . ."

Laviolette turned round. They hadn't dared touch the sycamore with its massive knots of twisted branches, like wooden muscles, reaching right over to the convent roofs. But all the rest – the lace tracery of the cloister, the seventeenth-century nativity scene angels mouldering away in the shadow of the walls – it had all been used as rubble to make a foundation for the floor of that smart municipal parking lot. They had, however, perpetuated the memory of the massacre with a fine neo-Provençal arch covered with new tiles, from which hung a wrought iron lantern.

"Did you know Bébé Fabre?" Laviolette asked.

"Of course I knew him! His sister's still here."

"What? What did you say? His sister?"

"Yairs! His sister. She was my poor mother's foster sister. She's almost 102! They left her a bit of the convent. Without that she'd have died, for sure. It's over there. That low door, just beside the arch. The maid'll answer the door. Just knock hard."

"I told you so!" Laviolette proclaimed to the gendarmes. "Fifty years is nothing at all."

A few women carrying baskets stopped out of curiosity to observe this deployment of gendarmes.

The men went and knocked on the door in the wall. It was solid, without unnecessary decoration, and had not closed properly for some time. The hand-shaped knocker was raised three times, disturbing some far-off sound of activity deep inside the building. They began to climb a staircase designed to serve fifty rooms and 200 metres of icy corridors. Three quarters of its original size had been lopped off. Someone higher up yelled at them to come in and go up the stairs. At last a head appeared over the balustrade, its features ravaged by hard times, dark circles around its eyes down to the wings of its nose. Seen from down below, it made quite a sight.

"Come up, gentlemen! Come up!" the head called once again. "Don't be afraid. I'm the housekeeper."

She must have been aware of the impression she made, but she was delighted by this unexpected visit: three agile gendarmes in single file, followed at a definite distance by an individual as broad as he was tall in overcoat and muffler.

At their request she led the way to a very small door in the corner of a high, white wall that cut through the 1.50-metre thickness of the old wall. They went through it as if entering an underground passage. The two tallest gendarmes had to bend a little to avoid hitting their heads.

It was a kitchen that smelled of pepper. The centenarian was sitting on a simple chair with her elbows solidly planted on the oilcloth covering a round table. At 102 years of age, the skin is smooth as yellowed ivory. It seems that erosion by the air had had enough time at last to do its work, whereas it is usually frustrated by the deplorable brevity of human life.

The old woman's spine was as bent as a bishop's crosier, but her eyes were lively and inquisitive. She was completely bald, without a single hair, apart from the thin, damp ends of a moustache that drooped each side of her sunken mouth.

"We could have killed her," Laviolette thought, "four of us bursting in like that. This ordinary visit, but with three gendarmes, looks awfully like a police search."

"Come in, gentlemen! Come in! I haven't set foot outside for more than fifteen years, but I know everything that's going on. Everything that's going on."

"Can she hear?" Laviolette whispered to the spinster housekeeper, who had had a tough life and who spent what was left of her unneeded affection on looking after the old institution.

"What?" she said.

"And why wouldn't I be able to hear?" the centenarian retorted.

Her voice tinkled up and down like broken crystal, as if she had come out of a musical box.

"Madame," Laviolette said, "I've come to talk with you about something that happened a long time ago."

The books in the attic were in their final resting place. When Bébé's library was knocked down with the rest, they had all been dumped here. They filled old chests, troughs, distillery flagons and even a very curious black coffin without a lid but with six handles decorated with two-headed eagles.

The wind of dead convents blew through the rafters, and the anachronistic sounds of the modern town seemed of no real importance around these 400-year-old rafters impregnated with the smell of nuns in black faille habits, which no amount of destruction could remove.

The gendarmes emptied boxes, looked at books, exclaimed at what they found.

"Don't let yourself get side-tracked," Chief Viaud said, ferreting around in his corner. "You're looking for only one thing, *Le Grand Albert*, and remember what the old lady said: it's not a big book and doesn't look impressive."

The noise of the town had died down and the sky had darkened when they finally came across it. Viaud was the one who found it – a slim brown volume, but a miserable, dirty brown – sitting in a bulbous chest of drawers beneath hundreds of love letters tied with pink and blue ribbon, more redolent of death than an old cemetery. They must have been bought with the piece of furniture and lain there ever since. No doubt Bébé Faure had slipped *Le Grand Albert*, a book of some value, underneath them, and had forgotten about it.

The three gendarmes and Laviolette stood gazing at the dirty old volume. It smelled of soot, and must have spent the best part of its life on the mantelpiece over the fireplace between the clock and the salt box.

Laviolette heaved a sigh of relief and put it in his pocket. Viaud went and gave an official receipt to the old lady.

They all returned to the van. Laviolette lay down on the stretcher and immediately fell asleep again, but his hand kept a firm hold on the book.

Night had fallen in Banon. Lights were on in every window of the police station. In the post-room, four gendarmes and the two inspectors Guyot and Leprince, who had been appointed to assist Laviolette, were studiously leaning over the large table in the middle.

"Ah!" Laviolette said jubilantly as he gazed at them, "This close collaboration between the National Gendarmerie and the CID is beautiful to behold. Just like the good old days. We should take a photo!"

At this rude remark, they all turned round.

"Chief! Come and look at this," the sergeant said. "I think we're on to something. You weren't held up by a snowdrift this morning, were you?"

"Yes, but . . ."

"Just after 'Capitaine'? On the north side of 'La Ramade'? Before Vachères?"

"Below Vachères," Viaud said. "That's right."

"It had been there since nine last night. We were told about it by an egg wholesaler who couldn't get through."

"OK," Viaud said, sitting down and taking off his cap.

The other gendarme looked a little taken aback by his indifference. Viaud noticed it.

"You mean that the murderer couldn't come from beyond Vachères? It's not exactly a vital clue."

"Hang on, Chief! We were working it out when you came back. If you'd just take a look . . ."

Viaud moved closer. His sergeant indicated the places with a ruler as he went along.

"All the statements agree," he said, "and also the work sheets of the Highways Department that we consulted. Yesterday evening, one hour before the murder was committed, all the road leading to the marquis' house, 'La Magnanerie,' were blocked by snowdrifts, except the one from Banon."

Viaud was about to speak.

"But even around Banon," the sergeant continued, "all the roads were blocked as well. Look! We've put crosses everywhere a snowdrift had formed: on the N 440 to the north at the Les Brieux hairpin bend; on the N 550 to the south in the Mares Basses gorges; on the forest road to Biscarle's place; on the D 5 towards Clos du Gardon; on the D 51 and the D 201 up near Riaille; on the D 12 at Grand-Valernes, below the distillery. That means that Banon and the scene of the crime were surrounded by snowdrifts. Therefore," he summed up triumphantly, "the murderer could not have come from anywhere but Banon."

"Except," Laviolette pointed out, "if he had hidden under the cedars at 'La Magnanerie' before the snowdrifts formed!"

"If that was the case," the sergeant replied quickly, "he would have got stuck in one of them making his escape after the crime. He wouldn't have risked waiting until this morning for someone to get him out. He would therefore have gone back on his tracks to Banon. If someone from outside the area spent the night here because of the snowdrifts, it won't be long before we hear about it. Someone would have seen him, either yesterday night or very early this morning."

"We pretty much suspect that the person responsible is in Banon," Viaud said. "Your reasoning is correct, but doesn't get us much further forward."

"Wait a moment!" Inspector Guyot said. "There's a series of facts here: this morning the ground under the cedars at 'La Magnanerie' was frozen, but yesterday evening it was still soft enough to leave wheel marks. Conditions were therefore ideal to make observations. We found ruts made by a car with chains on its wheels. The driver did several manoeuvres, perhaps hoping to cover his tracks. He didn't suspect that he was making our work much easier. These gentlemen," he said, indicating the gendarmes, "pointed out to us – as they usually do – that the circumference of the wheels can be worked out by measuring the distance separating two imprints of the clip on the chains. Are you with me?"

"Perfectly," replied Laviolette, who was beginning to see something.

"So! We've measured the distance between one imprint of the clip and another. We've calculated the circumference of the wheel. Then we've calculated the distance between the two front prints and between the two back ones, and finally – this was a bit more difficult, but the print of the chain key helped us here – the distance between the front and back wheel axis."

Inspector Guyot was cut short by the sergeant, a young man not yet thirty who could hardly contain his enthusiasm.

"We were also able to measure the depth of the imprints left by both the front and rear wheel axle units, and this is the conclusion we've come to: it can only be a Renault 4 CV."

"Which means," the phlegmatic inspector said, taking up where he left off, "that as access from Banon and to the scene of the crime was cut off by the snowdrifts, the tyre marks of the 4 CV found under the cedars must *necessarily* be those of a car that spent last night, the night of 21–22 December, in Banon or a nearby farm or hamlet. It could have left *after* the roads had been cleared, but it stayed there *before* that."

"The witnesses Bec and Biscarle hesitated when they were giving their description," Viaud said. "Do you remember? The night when the hippie was put in the freezer, they thought they saw a car turning in the square. Either a Volkswagen or a 4 CV . . ."

"And that's not all," Guyot said, "at some time or other, those old cars have always suffered at the hands of a mechanic who's used too much force on the thread of the sump plug, instead of screwing it by hand. And what happens? There's a tiny oil leak. This one was no exception. Under the cedars, where it was parked, there was a slight oil stain on the ground – and I do mean slight! We took a sample for analysis."

"Have the forensic boys from Criminal Records already got it?" Laviolette asked.

"They left with it this morning."

"But," one of the gendarmes said, "I thought that oils were all the same these days."

Inspector Guyot gave a wry smile.

"All new oils . . ." he said. "But our laboratories can compare the degree of wear in this sample with those we might need to take from a certain number of 4 CVs as the investigation proceeds."

Chief Viaud gave a huge sigh.

"Well! The way ahead is clear: check off all the 4 CVs in Banon and the surrounding countryside. Get warrants to go and search all of them. Check what all the owners were doing at the time . . ."

"Take oil samples from all the engines. But do you really think that there are many of these old cars in Banon?"

"There are quite a few on country roads," Viaud said, "partly for reasons of economy; partly to show that they're good drivers capable of getting about in the same vehicle for twenty years or more; partly for fear of the tax department; mostly to let the wife use the good car."

"There could be something like a dozen," the sergeant said.

"Let's try not to pin too much hope on all of this. The owner could have lent his car. It could have been stolen for the night and brought back in the morning. As for expert opinion about the oil . . . I have some idea of what a barrister might make of it in court . . ."

"Why don't you sit down, Superintendent?" the sergeant said.

"I'm sorry," Laviolette said. "If I sit down, I'll fall asleep . . ."

Two gendarmes had already left for the communications room to search central records for all types of Renault 4 CVs on the vehicle registration documents for Banon.

"No. Believe me gentlemen," Laviolette said, "the truth is in here!"

He waved the brown book, which had still not lost its sooty smell.

"I'm about to get on to it right now."

"I'll have someone drive you back," Viaud said.

"You must be joking. It's 500 metres . . ."

And he left. The gendarmes and the inspectors remained silent. When they were sure that Laviolette was well on his way, all of the men, none of whom were over thirty-five, heaved a collective sigh of relief.

"How much sleep do you think he's had in the last three days?" Viaud asked.

"I don't know. Five, six hours . . ."

"Plus two half-hours in the police van. I bet you . . ."

"Don't bother," Guyot said. "Do you know his motto? '*No delay* and *no let-up* are the lifeblood of the police force'.* When he's on a case, you have to drag him off it bit by bit, like a tick from a dog! And what's more, it's his friend who's just been killed."

"All the same," Viaud said, "I'd still like to take the case over from him."

He went towards the communications room. What he didn't mention either was that he had had scarcely an hour's more sleep in three days than Laviolette.

If they went by the look of him, a police patrol would have arrested Laviolette on the spot. He was dragging his feet, lurching from one tree to another, but without touching them. Several of the hypothetical 4 CVs came close to him on the square as they jolted along, finding their way home, all making the same dismal noise with their chains: tacatac . . . tacataca . . ."

Rosemonde was waiting with her chin on her hand.

"Well! What a fine sight you are!"

"Have they all gone?" Laviolette asked.

"Who do you mean?"

"The card players."

"Of course. It's eleven o'clock. And look at that! The snow is starting to fall."

"Just like me," Laviolette said. "Pity. I'd like to have had a talk with those gentlemen."

Rosemonde shrugged her shoulders.

"He'd like to have had a talk. If I don't give him a hand, he won't even make it to the top of the stairs."

"Rosemonde of my heart! I'm not joking when I call you that. I've never been so glad to come back to a house. It's because you're here . . ."

"You don't mean . . ."

He shook his head.

* This is Laviolette's version of the old proverb: Ploughing and grazing are the lifeblood of France.

"It's not for selfish reasons," he said. "It's because . . . and you'll understand this . . . they've killed my friend. Did you know that they've killed my friend?"

"I know that someone else has been killed."

"Well, you're going to help me. There's still something I have to do tonight."

"Sit down. I'll make you a nice cup of strong coffee."

"I'd like that. But without sitting down. If I sit down, I'll fall asleep."

He leaned on the mantelpiece, brought the lamp closer, opened the book and began to leaf through it. He could hardly remain standing. Rosemonde kept her eye on him, ready to grab him if he fell. The smell of soot from the book grew stronger and stronger; the kind of soot that comes from fireplaces where rags and all sorts of revolting things were burned, but those who knew about them are long buried under gravestones in family vaults. Laviolette unselfconsciously licked his thumb to turn the pages. He detected a taste of stewed viper overlaid with the lemon liqueur witches used in the old days to disguise the taste. Rosemonde drew back slightly.

Suddenly she heard him give a huge sigh. He straightened up a little. The fatigue seemed to fade from his face, but there was a look of horrible surprise in his eyes, which did not disappear until he closed the book again.

"Rosemonde, I know . . ." was all he said.

He went over to the telephone, took a notebook from his pocket, looked up a number and rang it.

"Hello! Combassive. Yes, it's me, and I know it's late. And yes, I know I'm calling you at home. Are you watching TV? No, I'm sorry, I was joking. I need some search warrants. I can't get them here, but you can. The judge? Go and wake him up . . . in Digne. He'll be asleep again in no time. Have them brought to me by police courier. Yes. As soon as possible. How many? . . ."

He put his hand over the receiver.

"Rosemonde, how many truffle-tree owners are there in Banon?"

"I don't know. Thirty? Forty?" she suggested.

"Fifty!" Laviolette said into the phone. "No, of course not! I'm asleep on my feet. Would I be joking? Listen, could you do me a favour, even though it's outside your brief? I'm afraid I might collapse before I can do it myself. Yes? Thanks. Would you call Criminal Records. Tell them that I want the forensic boys here as early as possible tomorrow morning. At five or six, if they can make it. Yes, I'm well aware that it will be two days before Christmas and that people are on leave. As a matter of fact, I was going to spend Christmas Eve with my friend who's just been murdered. Yes, all right . . . And many thanks for doing this for me on trust."

He hung up and put the book back in his pocket.

"Do you want me to help you upstairs?"

"Careful, Rosemonde! I could say yes . . ."

"You could . . . And why not?"

She looked at him with a dry smile.

"And what would you say to that?"

"Ah!" she said. "Who knows? I'll tell you when we get there . . ."

XX

LAVIOLETTE WOKE UP IN HIS BEDROOM AT EIGHT O'CLOCK, his head as clear as a bell. The air smelled of truffles, the sheets of lavender, and he the scent of Rosemonde. It was snowing. He reached out for the book on the bedside table and reread the passage. He was flabbergasted. He could hardly believe his eyes.

"There must be two things," he said out loud. "Firstly, he must be mad, and then he must need money . . . someone with a 4 CV, truffle trees and big money worries . . . You must admit that helps identify the problem . . ."

"What do you want me to admit, Superintendent?" said Rosemonde, fresh as a daisy as she came in with the breakfast tray. "I knocked, but you didn't hear me."

From eight in the morning until eleven at night she addressed him formally.

"Everyone's waiting for you downstairs," she said.

"Who's everyone?"

"Everyone! A courier from Digne. I'm warming him up with cups of coffee. Chief Viaud and the two inspectors. Then there are the journalists. They never stop asking questions."

"Answer them!" Laviolette said. "I definitely don't want them making things up! And ask the chief, the inspectors and the courier to come up."

"Oh! I nearly forgot. There are also the three forensic men from Criminal Records, who've just arrived."

"Well, Rosemonde, he said, "it's time to open shop again!"

"Do you want me to send all these people up?"

"All except the journalists. See if you can amuse them."

The steps shook as they all trooped up the stairs. Although it was a very big room, it was soon full of people.

"A council of war," Laviolette said looking pleased. "It's rather like Louis XIV on his deathbed, but fear not. This is just to save time."

He signed for the search warrants.

Rosemonde brought seats for everyone. They were those lovely green and yellow straw-bottomed chairs which were always found lined up against the wall in Provençal bedrooms in the old days. They were only sat on to keep vigil over the bodies of the dead. They used to last a hundred years.

The forensic boys from Criminal Records were straining at the leash as usual. They were dying to find a lead to bring the murderer to court. The three of them were so conscious of their irresistible power that Laviolette sometimes wished they would fail.

"Gentlemen," he said, "I think we're beginning to identify the problem, which doesn't mean, of course, that we've solved it . . . And it's taken seven bodies to get us to this point. You must admit that it's nothing to get very excited about . . ."

They were all looking at the dirty book lying on its own on the marble top of the bedside table. Laviolette followed their gaze.

"No!" he said. "For the time being, don't expect me to tell you what I've found in it. I'm not keen on seeing you making fun of me to my face."

"The murderer must know that you have this book," Inspector Guyot responded matter-of-factly. "He could try to kill you to get it back. The risk is . . ."

"Then you can pray for me!" Laviolette said, interrupting him. "But let's cut out the humour. I imagine that, like me, you haven't had much sleep. So? Who's going to begin?"

They all looked at each other.

"We have the results of the autopsies on the first six victims," Guyot said. "Do you want me to read them to you?"

"Just give me the main points. Give me a general summary of what's in them. I think that although they're highly significant, for once they're not going to be the deciding factor."

"The five victims," Guyot continued, "had their throats cut with a sharp tool that was neither a razor, a knife nor any kind of surgical instrument. In his conclusion, Dr Rabinovitch is inclined to think that it was, and I quote: 'a cobbler's knife, used to cut out crêpe rubber soles. Something solid and made of really good steel. It was probably old, with the end of the blade slightly curved in a sickle shape, and the point sharpened on all sides.' The victims," Guyot went on, "were strung up by their ankles and completely drained of blood. Shortly before they died, they had smoked pot, had a good meal and drunk marc brandy."

"Did you say five?"

"Yes, I did. The sixth victim was killed in a different way. By a blunt instrument: an adjustable spanner, probably fairly long. And he hadn't smoked pot or drunk a drop of alcohol."

"Who was it?" Laviolette asked.

"The one called Jeremy Piochet."

Laviolette recalled Claire's face with its limpid eyes and innocent expression. He could see her rather reserved figure in the Scottish coat – the envy of the Deputy Public Prosecutor – but which nonetheless showed off the smooth line of her hips. She was on the lookout for the murderer. She had promised to kill him . . .

Laviolette had an uneasy feeling.

"I'd like . . ." he began saying, but then changed his mind. "Please go on."

"That's just about all. Given the decomposition of the bodies, one couldn't ask for . . . The time of death for each of them more or less corresponds, Dr Rabi says, to the time they disappeared. They had done a lot of walking in their lives. Barefoot. The callous on their heels was abnormally thick. Despite the pot, they were in very good physical condition."

"Was there enough blood left for analysis?"

Guyot delved into the dossier and looked for the end of the report.

"Yes, for three of them: the most recent, and especially for the body in the deep freeze. As for the others . . . the state they were in . . ."

The chief took a notebook out of his bag.

"For our part," he said, "up to now we have identified nine owners of 4 CV, in Banon or the farms and hamlets around the town. Two of them are out of contention. The first owner was with seven other people at a wake of an uncle who died at Varages, in the Var. The second car has been up on blocks at Martel's garage for a week, waiting for a standard replacement. He's the parish priest . . ."

"Right. And the seven others?"

"Here are the other seven."

Viaud got up to hand him the list.

"In the present circumstances," he said, "I preferred leaving the investigation of these seven until I had spoken to you."

Laviolette, who was going through the list, gave him a penetrating look.

"I think you did the right thing," he said.

"We," Guyot said, "that is, Leprince and myself went up to Montsalier to question the hippies."

"What do you mean question? Don't tell me they answered you?"

Guyot and Leprince looked guilty.

"There were three girls and only one guy," Guyot said. "We'd put dirty old clothes on and brought some grog . . . We had to make a slight personal sacrifice . . ."

"My poor lads! You must be worn out."

"Well, not as much as all that, all things considered. They may be hippies, but those German and Dutch girls are still practical. They had excellent duvets."

Laviolette raised his eyes to heaven. Where were the good old days when witnesses were persuaded to answer with threats or even the odd kick in the pants? And when they hesitated for too long, we described the heavens or the pit of hell opening for them. Today they make love to them. What times we live in!

"I hope that at least you didn't sacrifice yourselves in vain?"

"Not entirely. Around morning we offered them a joint, as they'd been out of them for three days."

"Watch what you're saying!" Laviolette exclaimed.

Guyot shrugged his shoulders. These policemen from the sub-prefecture should really be brought up to date. He threw an opened packet of flat cigarettes on the bed. Laviolette sniffed them with great distaste. It made him want to roll one of his own.

"They're a substitute," Leprince said. "One of the lab. boys thought it up one day when he had nothing to do. They're made from dried clematis and wormwood. They're disgusting!"

"But the best thing about it," Guyot said, following on, "is that after ten minutes they were in pot paradise, which they described to us in full detail."

"They were well away. It was then they told us that there was a hippie trail that went all around the world. It's not on the map, and only the initiated know the itinerary. It also indicates the locations of pot suppliers. And Banon was one of them."

"Who?" Laviolette asked.

"They didn't know," Guyot said. "That's the truth! They didn't know. And we went all out, I can tell you! Didn't we, Leprince?"

"I'll say!" Leprince replied, nodding his head in confirmation of it.

"Chief," Laviolette asked, "do you think that cannabis could be grown in the Banon area and you wouldn't be aware of it?"

Viaud shook his head.

"The colour of cannabis is so distinctive in our region that just a clump of it would stand out like a matador's red cape in a green field."

"Excuse me, Chief," Guyot said, "but the narcotics squad has two precedents on file: one in the département of the Va, and the other in the Aude. It's a matter of large areas. One or two hundred plants, not in groups, but carefully hidden at random . . . over 100 hectares . . . For

153

example: among lavender, potatoes . . . or near those huts with brambles around them, that we know so well . . . They're as high as thistles, as tall hemlock . . ."

"But they have to be watered," Laviolette objected.

"No doubt. But do you think anyone would notice a man on a tractor pulling one of those copper sulphate spraying machines with only water in it going from one field to another?"

Leprince supported him.

"The two girls seemed sure of what they were saying. But they said to us several times, 'Only the initiated know. We don't. We're relative newcomers.'"

Laviolette thought for a few moments in silence as he rolled his first cigarette of the day.

"Right then," he said at last. "This is what we're looking for: a man whose property is crossed by the invisible hippie trail; a man with lands extensive enough to hide a few hundred cannabis plants, if necessary . . ."

"There are so few now who are still farmers," Viaud said, "that they all have more than 300 hectares . . ."

"The person in question," Laviolette continued, "is mad, but also intelligent and calculating. You could say, a bit like all of us. That's not exactly going to give us an Identikit picture of him. But in addition, he drives one of the 4 CVs on the list; he has truffle trees and he needs a lot of money . . ."

"Why so much?" Viaud asked.

"If I knew that, I'd know who the murderer was. He must be fairly involved with the Crédit Agricole . . ."

"They all are," Viaud sighed. "A search of the bank records wouldn't be a great deal of help. But . . . how do you know that he has a truffle wood?"

Laviolette evaded the question.

"In short," he said, "although his method may be unusual, the person we're looking for commits the most straightforward of crimes: he kills to get extra income."

"But this unusual method . . . Are you the only one to know about it?"

"For the simple reason I explained to you," Laviolette said. "And now, if you don't mind, I'm going to shower, shave and get dressed."

"And what about us?" the three forensic men from Criminal Records said in a chorus.

"Ah, you! It's true. I am inclined to forget you . . ."

But there you are. Nothing could be done about it. Once again, they were the ones in the force who'd hit the jackpot . . . the science boys. He waited until Viaud, Guyot and Leprince had gone out of the room before giving his instructions to the three musketeers.

It lifted his spirits to see Digne again. It was definitely the town he most loved. Perhaps because it only developed very slowly. It was the town most like Montaigne in the world. He rejoiced in having his house, his garden and his cemetery plot here. A wave of nostalgia swept over him as the old courthouse building came into view. He could feel his heart beating as he knocked at the Examining Magistrate's door.

The office was still the same, but Judge Chabrand had disappeared into the wide world searching for some manifestation or other of the absolute. In this haunted dreamer's* place sat a normal, friendly and convivial man who enjoyed complete peace of mind. He asked Laviolette to sit down, folded his hands and listened to the end.

"But this is an incredible story you're telling me!" he exclaimed, hardly believing what he had heard. "Are you sure of the conclusions you've drawn?"

"Three forensic men from Criminal Records are doing the necessary investigations right now. You can see how cautious and questioning I've been; how much I've doubted my own assumptions. I didn't even tell them what I was looking for. I simply said that the tests should include *all* reactions."

---

* See Pierre Magnan's *Le Sang des Atrides* [*The Blood of the Atrides*], Fayard, 1977.

The magistrate nodded. "Your profession and mine are becoming more and more difficult," he said.

"We're the ones," Laviolette said, "who are becoming more and more difficult . . ."

"Well then," the magistrate asked, "shall I issue a warrant for you?"

Laviolette thought hard before replying. He got up and went to the window where he had so often stood and gazed at the roofs of Digne with Judge Chabrand. After a few moments he came back to the magistrate.

"Two!" he said.

XXI

THEY WERE NOT IN THEIR PLACES FOR THE USUAL GAME OF cards. They didn't have the heart for it. They were sitting around Rosemonde's stove in a frosty, fearful circle. Outside, the weather came in waves of driving snow or rain, sometimes melting, sometimes freezing. Their feet inside their shoes had not been warm since they got out of bed, when three young men in black jackets had presented each of them with a fine legal piece of paper authorising Criminal Records to carry out investigations in their truffle woods.

"If you ask me," Polycarpe Bleu said, "I'm sure they're looking for foreign bombs."

"Hell! Maybe they are," exclaimed Sidoine Pipeau.

"There's no maybe about it. You believe everything you're told. They make me laugh with their rocket silos. What about the others? They've all got them now. It's full of 'em around here and up there. Riddled with 'em!"

Bleu with his impressive tic didn't speak very often, but when he opened his mouth he was straight away Cassandra on the ramparts of Ilium.

"The Russians made some that really penetrate."

"Penetrate?" Pascalon Bayle said, allowing himself to express a doubt on the subject.

"Exactly! Penetrate! And the size of a goose's egg! In all kinds of shapes. There could be one in the football the kids play with. Why, there could be one in that knotty beech tree root you left in Le Deffens woods. Do you remember, Sidoine? Three years ago. The one you couldn't break. The one that weighed maybe six hundred kilos. Do you remember? Maybe that's the reason. Who would have thought of a beech root?"

"Oh, you!" said Rosemonde, who was listening with her chin on her hands and her chest resting on the counter.

"That's because I notice things. I'm far-sighted."

"Sure!" Rosemonde said. "Be careful! There may be one in the sugar you put in your coffee."

"Don't joke about it!"

"To stop a donkey from braying, you need a good bale of hay," Rosemonde said with a sigh.

"A bale of hay. There you are! But you won't find anything even if you look. It's hay. It's really and truly hay. You can spread it. Nothing there! You can even give this hay to your animals, so you see what I mean?"

He had them spellbound. They almost forgot the reason why they had given up their sacrosanct game of cards. The only thing that made them waver somewhat was his tic, which broke out twice as he was speaking.

"And what about the Americans. They make them hardly as big as that!" he exclaimed waving his two clenched fists together in front of him. "And they've been circling. Out there in the sky. For maybe five years now. Just about on a level with the Lure mountains."

His index finger traced the movement of a satellite circling the Earth. Then he stopped suddenly, without finishing what he was saying. He had just caught sight of Laviolette who had tiptoed in and was hanging his coat up on the hook while making encouraging signs to him.

"Go on! Go on! Please don't interrupt anything on my account."

He sat down in the middle of the group, which pushed back hastily, giving him a wide berth.

"Please! Please! Don't move so far away. Stay near the heat. I really don't need so much space."

He calmly began rolling a cigarette.

"Well now? Aren't there any cards this evening?"

He was obviously in such good form that it made Rosemonde feel uneasy.

As for the seven card players, they were squirming on their straw-bottomed chairs. None of them wanted to be the first to reply. One was cleaning out the stem of his pipe; the other was warming his hand at the oil stove. Omer Bleu picked up a copy of *Le Provençal* and opened it at the local news page. Virgile Bleu was unashamedly picking his nose. Albert Pipeau was whittling a toothpick out of a matchstick, still smiling the smile of a man who has women galore. Pascalon Bayle was noisily sipping his coffee from the glass.

They all had that open, guileless, direct look they had long ago been taught to present when questioned.

"Just look at them!" Laviolette thought. "You'd think they had consciences as clear as the day."

He studied all their faces, none of them moving a muscle.

"All things considered," he said, "you made the right decision not to start a game. I've a little story to tell you and I think it will interest all of you. Rosemonde! Give me a brandy and water, will you? I'm dying of thirst!"

He leaned back and relaxed as he lit his hand-rolled cigarette.

"Just lift the catch on the lock, Rosemonde. In case some journalist tries to . . ."

"I've got a headache," Rosemonde declared. "I'm going up to my room. Call me when you've finished, so that I can close up."

"Right! There we are! Now we can relax: all together in pleasant company. I could, of course, have called you all down to the police station, but that wouldn't have been the right thing to do. I'd prefer us to work all this out together – in a friendly way. All right! I'm not going to beat about the bush. It will put you more at your ease. You remember those six hippies we found? Five in the Protestant tomb and one in the

Hôtel des Fraches' deep freeze? You remember them, don't you? And you also remember the Marquis de Brèdes, who was killed two nights ago? Well, all these murders are the work of one and the same person. A person who is right here amongst us this evening . . ."

"Is that so!" said Omer Bleu.

He was the only one who said anything. You have to realise that they were acting like true inhabitants of the Basses-Alpes. They had received Laviolette's revelation without changing expression, without even clearing their throats or shuffling their feet. You'd have taken them for a studious class listening to a maths problem being explained. The only difference was that Omer Bleu's "Is that so!" meant "Get lost!"

"Therefore," Laviolette went on, "all I have to do now is guess which one of you it is. But, never fear! It's only a question of time and patience . . . And by the way, I owe you an apology. I should have given you the search warrants in person. No need to worry though: my men are used to this kind of work, and they won't damage anything."

Omer Bleu shook his long head with its oilcloth cap.

"No damage! No damage! Looking for truffles is a delicate business. If they cut our chains . . . I personally have great reservations . . ."

Laviolette clearly saw in their eyes what they were thinking: "The first person who gives way and asks a question has had it." Their mouths were shut more tightly than a money bag.

"I can see," Laviolette continued, "that you're dying to know how I arrived at that conclusion. Am I right? You're dying to know? Admit it!"

The only response to his question came from the oil stove spluttering and the wind lapping under the door.

"I won't keep you in suspense. The night the hippie's body was put in the freezer, Biscarle and Jules Bec, who were going to the fire station, saw a 4 CV in the square. And the night the Marquis de Brèdes was murdered, we have identified the killer's car, which had been hidden under the cedars. It also was a 4 CV. As the murderer leaves his signature in the way he commits all his crimes, the same person, i.e. the man in the 4 CV, is guilty of the seven murders. Are you with me? All right.

Now follow what I say carefully. We have identified nine 4 CVs in Banon. One belongs to Séraphin Calandre, the metal worker. On the night Brèdes was killed, he was at the wake of an uncle who died in Varages. The second belongs to the parish priest. It's been up on blocks in Martel's garage since 15 December.

"The engine's missing," Sidoine blurted out.

That harmless sentence lightened the atmosphere a little. It was like a valve releasing the tension in the room.

"That's right. The new engine hasn't arrived yet. The gendarmes found the third car in a gypsy camp at Le Plan-de-Trabuc. It hasn't any wheels, doors, battery or distributor. It's being used as a rabbit hutch. The fourth belongs to a dead man, Gabriel Coupier, and is in his shed. His widow washes it every day while shedding copious tears. 'Poor Gabriel. He was so fond of his car!'"

Omer Bleu looked doubtful.

"No," Laviolette continued. "It's on blocks too, without any oil or petrol. We checked. No-one has used it since Gabriel died."

He raised his hand with the fingers wide apart.

"Five," he said. "That leaves five – the five who are on our list. And I stress that this list is in alphabetical order, and is not at all in any order of preference. Would you hand it around, gentlemen. Come on, take it! Don't feel embarrassed."

But they showed a great reluctance to take it.

"No! No! Read it to us," Alyre Morelon said, "it's easier that way."

Laviolette unfolded the sheet of paper and read out the list:

Bayle, Pascalon

Bleu, Polycarpe

Morelon, Alyre

Pipeau, Albert

Pipeau, Sidoine

Whereupon Omer Bleu and Virgile Bayle suddenly found their voices again, overjoyed that the two of them got about in old Dauphines that practically dragged along the ground, their shock absorbers were so worn.

"So what does that mean?" Omer said.

"That means there's a coincidence!" exclaimed Virgile. "The only 4 CVs left are all here!"

Laviolette then explained to them about the snowdrifts surrounding Banon on the night that Brèdes was murdered.

"That rules out anything coming from outside Banon . . ."

To tell the truth, there weren't only aces in his hand. There was another possibility: a 4 CV not identified by the gendarmes that could have been hidden away in the garage of some holiday home closed for the year, to which X had the key. He could have used the car just on these occasions. Besides, the motor oil taken from the ground under the cedars could not be identified. The report stated that it was "a mixture of oil-change products'. It was still the case that the user of the 4 CV had to own truffle woods and was present at the gathering of war veterans at Brèdes' house, otherwise the marquis would not have been murdered.

Laviolette looked each of them full in the face, one after the other, but it would be difficult to find anyone who looked more normal, ordinary and impassive than they did. Which one was the killer? What "reasonable" face did he present to the world? Did he fill his pipe with a hand that never trembled? Drink in moderation? Drive well to the right? Search for his truffles? Store his six or seven kegs of lavender essence to sell next year if the price was higher?

They should all have been asking, "But what on earth are you looking for in our truffle woods?"

Nothing. Not a word.

He finished his cigarette. Outside, the muted moaning of the wind rose and fell as it blew through the badly joined boards in lofts, against loose shutters with rusty bolts, and over the metallic squawks of disorientated weathercocks.

"Which one of you?" Laviolette said, breaking the silence. "I admit I don't know. In theory I should exclude Omer Bleu and Virgile Bayle who both have Dauphines . . . But how can I be sure that someone didn't lend them a 4 CV? Oh, I know! You're all brothers who don't get on with each other. But to what extent? Sitting there in front of me, you all stick together. Let me put this to you quite plainly: I have here before me a murderer and six people who know it!"

He gave them their first chance to say something by stopping and rolling another cigarette. There was not a tremor in the assembled company.

"I have the feeling you're protesting," he said with rather heavy irony. "And yet, living together for such a long time, you must know who owns the cobbler's knife? You must know who owns the key to the Protestant tomb. You must know who had big enough money worries to grow a few cannabis plants in his spare time to sell to passing hippies. And above all, you must know which of you owns a 'spell-caster's veil' – the one I saw on the day Brèdes was killed. Isn't that so? Now gentlemen, if I wasn't born and bred in the Basses-Alpes myself, if I hadn't had a grandmother who was a walking encyclopaedia, I would never know that! But you know. You know all that, don't you? You know?"

No, they didn't know anything. They stared into Laviolette's eyes as if he were telling them a fantastically interesting story and they were dying to know the ending. They didn't turn to each other; they withdrew into themselves. Although they were all sitting around the stove, there suddenly seemed to be a huge distance between them.

"But there is something that you don't know, or at least that six out of seven of you don't know: it's *why* he kills! You don't know that he's mad! We're dealing with a madman here. Is that starting to sink into your thick skulls?"

But Laviolette's audience showed remarkable self-control. He stared at them sitting there right under his nose, but all he could see were blank faces, severe expressions, distant gazes. They no longer even pretended to be smoking. They were all trying not to appear mad, and succeeding.

"I'll stay at the police station all day tomorrow," Laviolette said, "and I can be reached by phone. If, by any chance, one of you should suddenly get an attack of remorse and have some belated scruples . . . Well, there you are. I've told you everything for this evening. But", he said brightly, "don't let that stop us from having our game of cards!"

With a wide sweep of his arm, he indicated the tables and the decks of cards. He was met with sullen faces all round. They got up together, straightened their caps, walked over and took their sheepskin jackets off the peg.

They made their excuses . . . well, not really . . . They hadn't the heart for it and, besides, it was late, and tomorrow was Christmas Eve, it would be a long night and . . .

They were already crossing the threshold. The wind made the juniper bushes in the parking areas look larger. Fine needles blown off the branches flew through the gateway and settled on the men's coats.

"Wait!" Laviolette said, as if he suddenly remembered a detail he had forgotten to mention. "It does rather bother me that I can't offer you any kind of protection . . . Unfortunately, I don't have enough men, and there are too many of you. Anyway . . . try to be careful. Because this murderer, whom none of you know, could take it into his head . . . mistakenly, of course! But how can you tell, when you're dealing with a madman? They're clever. If you ask me, he's already picked out who among you will weaken and come to see me tomorrow . . . What am I saying, tomorrow! Why not very soon? There's a telephone at Rosemonde's. I can be contacted at any time. And in secret . . . anonymously. Now just imagine if the killer thought that! I don't think you'd be in the same league! Would you like me to tell you how my friend the Marquis des Brèdes died?"

They intimated they did not by hunching their necks into their collars. That didn't matter. He told them regardless. The darkness. The lights out. The sound of the cedars. The glug of the carotid artery spurting blood. How he had blocked it with his thumb. The figure in the fearful black veil stopping for a moment in the doorway, wondering if it wasn't going to kill him too . . . The incredible time it took to reach the telephone with his friend held in his arm. His hand covered in blood to the wrist like a red lace glove. He surprised himself with this onrush of lyricism.

"This murderer," he went on, while they were going out in single file, "has already killed seven people, with some relish, it would seem . . . He knows that one of you, or several, represent a latent danger to him. So . . ."

There seemed to be a slight disturbance in the orderly exit of the seven men: a kind of ebb and flow from the front to the back, then from the back to the front again. Each of them had his hands deep in his pockets and his cap squarely on his head. They all went out, looking as severe as judges. Laviolette had pulled on his overcoat and wound his muffler around his neck. He went with them, insistent, persuasive, in the unlikely hope that one of them would finally grab him by the collar or stick his fist under his nose to stop his endless talk.

But no! They continued to mull over the arguments for and against. Yet, that night they would have to make up their minds, and quickly. The murderer . . . and the only thing you could be certain of was that you yourself were not the one . . . the twisting lane with no streetlight where you lived . . . The farm, at Pampaligouste . . . The pretty villa, but at the end of a dark pathway bordered with pines and their very murky shade . . . All that was enough to make you think hard.

There in the little square with the fountain waited the two Dauphines without shock absorbers and the five 4 CVs, all a uniform grey-blue, having been out in the weather for so many seasons. And especially one among them with a bumper tied up with wire, the left headlamp hanging out of its socket like a gouged eye . . .

They stood in a circle in front of their cars, freezing cold, stamping their feet, in a state of utter confusion.

"There's only one thing to do . . ." Omer Bleu said finally. "And that's to see each other home."

"What do you mean, see each other home?"

"We all leave together," Omer Bleu explained. "First we go with Pascalon Bayle to Le Largue, 'cos it's the furthest . . . We all wait together until he goes in and closes the door . . . After that . . . It's no concern of ours! We leave there, still all together, we take Sidoine Pipeau to La Mute, then Albert Pipeau to La Confrérie, and so on . . . And the last two are my . . . brother and Alyre Morelon, who live almost opposite each other . . ."

"Yes! But these last two . . . that's the whole point. What if one kills the other?"

"Listen! Mind what you're saying!"

"No, but just supposing."

"If one kills the other," Omer Bleu explained, "he won't get away with it, because we'll know straight away that it's him!"

You should have seen them standing around their cars, which suddenly seemed like deathtraps. You should have seen them: mature, experienced men, hands in pockets, stamping about in the cold night wind.

"They're scared witless!" Laviolette thought. "I've already got that far."

He watched them with great interest as they calculated their chances of escaping from the killer.

Francine was very careful not to react when she heard the news from Alyre. In the blackness of the winter night behind closed shutters, no-one could see her grow pale, thank God.

"But why one of them?"

"Search me!" Alyre said. "Firstly, they say that the murderer's car is a 4 CV, and only ours are suspect."

"There you are! Haven't I always told you to get rid of that 4 CV. To take my Renault 6 and buy me a Porsche!"

Alyre went on regardless.

"It must also be a question of money, because they asked the Crédit Agricole for information about all our accounts."

"Our accounts! But they don't have the right to do that!"

"The right, my poor Francine! With their legal warrants, as they call them . . . They're already digging up our truffle woods! Now do you still think they haven't the right?"

"It's not you?" Francine said.

She didn't believe a word of it, but had to pretend that her teeth were chattering and that she was scared stiff. She felt him shrugging his shoulders as he lay on the pillow.

"How could it be me?" he said. "Big money worries . . . You know that I don't have any . . . But the superintendent seems to think that we all know something and that the killer knows it, and that one day soon he'll cut the throat of another victim . . . or two. We were so scared this evening that we saw each other home. He's a laugh, that policeman. How can he expect us to know anything? Do *you* know who inherited the *Uillaoude*'s veil? Though I must say that I've been wondering about that for the last fortnight. The murderer, Francine, is the man who hurt my Roseline. You see . . . I did the right thing locking her up. And what's more . . . do *you* know who needs a lot of money? Do *you* know who inherited the key to the Protestant tomb? Have you seen one of us mad enough to grow that grass, that grass . . . you know . . . um . . ."

"Cannabis . . ." Francine whispered.

She turned on to her side and managed to hide her terror by giving a big, tired sigh.

"Be quiet and go to sleep," she said pretending to yawn. "We'll talk about it in the morning."

But she curled herself up tight as a shiver of dread travelled through her body. She could still hear the voice of that man the last time she had allowed him to make love to her, despite the revulsion she felt. "Francine, you're making me bankrupt! But you're the only one I love!"

That was nearly six months ago. Whenever she happened to come across him, he would whisper to her, "I'm saving up, Francine. I'm saving up. Next time it will be a diamond brooch. You'd like that, a diamond brooch. You'd do it for a diamond brooch, eh? Tell me you would." "We'll see," she would say, and go on her way.

Lying in the conjugal bed, she very, very carefully took off the ring she had loved so much. Now it burned her finger. She placed it on the bedside table with the pearl necklace and the wristwatch set with small diamonds, letting her hand rest for a few seconds on the little pile of jewels. So much for the ring, so much for the necklace, so much for the watch . . . It was a chore each time she had to make love . . . But what pleasure can a man take with a woman who feels none? "Men always believe . . ." And now, since the police had narrowed it down to the five, she was sure it was him.

And the key to the Protestant tomb! Of course she knew about it. One day when she was there, he had taken down an enormous key which was hanging on the nail that held the Post Office calendar. He laughed as he said to her "Look Francine, that's Bluebeard's Key". He must have convinced himself of that little by little, wondering for a long time what use he could make of it. Then at last he knew . . .

Her thoughts were racing. "He'll confess. They'll get to me. They'll discover the shop in Marseilles where he bought my jewels . . . I'll lose people's respect. And then, Paul . . . Oh, my God! Paul!"

Paul, her son, her pride and joy . . . The career she dreamed of for him, the advantageous marriage, the high position in society . . . All that cut off before it had begun by a mother called as principal witness in court . . . Perhaps as an accomplice. She hastily withdrew her hand from the jewels.

She had to give them back to him! Not just get rid of them . . . They should be found at his place during a search. If they were found with him, he could call Francine as a witness as much as he liked, no-one would believe him. On the other hand, they were such lovely jewels. But there was Paul!

Francine's heart alternated wildly between her love of jewellery and her love for her son. She spent a very bad night listening to the wind; but in the morning her mind was made up.

XXII

ON THE MORNING OF 24 DECEMBER, THE FORENSIC BOYS
from the Criminal Records Office, with their gear across their shoulders, resumed the search which had been interrupted the evening before when night fell.

All of Banon took it in relays to hang around the fields that the gendarmes had cordoned off.

Incensed, the inhabitants of Banon moaned to each other. "Our truffle woods have never been so well protected against pilfering. But what are they looking for?"

"More bodies!" was the usual reply.

Inspired by the unburied bodies in the Protestant tomb, the popular imagination hoped to discover something even better. The journalists spent their time questioning people who knew nothing, but who had an amazing amount to report.

As he had announced to the men at Rosemonde's, Laviolette stayed by the phone at the police station. Gendarmes had kept the five suspects under discreet surveillance all night. Their findings were summed up in three words: nothing to report.

At eleven o'clock a specialist from Marseilles who had come to collect the samples also contributed some extra details. Firstly, Laviolette had been right. The prints in the tomb precinct of feet in socks but no shoes were no help. The socks, which had been identified, were the commonest you could find, sold in all the country markets. At least a hundred inhabitants of Banon put them on every morning. There was one thing, however: caught on the prickles of a thistle were one or two infinitesimally tiny filaments, about the same thickness as gossamer. They had been identified under the electron microscope as coming from threads of woven material, but they did not match up with any of the huge number of samples available. They would seem to be genuine pure wool, i.e. not mixed with any kind of cotton or artificial fibre. It would seem to be a material that was either rare or very old.

"Oh! And another thing," the specialist said, giving a slight cough. "Dr Rabinovitch has some doubt about his original opinion. He'll send you the official results, of course, but the examination of the Marquis des Brèdes' body and the wound already leads him to think that the murder weapon, and most likely that used in the other killings, may not be a cobbler's knife. It's more likely to be a special knife used for sticking pigs . . ."

"Ah! Right," Laviolette sighed. "It did seem to me at the time that our Dr Rabinovitch was being a little too optimistic . . ."

At lunchtime they brought him a serving of braised beef, which he heated on the oil stove, and a bottle of the Château de Pinet recommended by Rosemonde. His meal was accompanied by the rustle of ten kilos of papers and photos he looked through as he ate and drank. The horribly realistic photo of the interior of the tomb with the bodies laid out in a line was propped up against the telephone in front of him. The sight never left his mind as he pensively ate his braised beef.

At three o'clock the truffle hunters came to report on their findings, and to say that they were going back to Marseilles. They had unintentionally dug up a few truffles, which they had scrupulously left where they were.

"I'll inform the owners," Chief Viaud said.

At eight o'clock in the evening Laviolette threw in the towel. None of the card players had called. None of them had turned up. In that case, the only thing to do, he thought, was to wait for the results of the tests, which would take three or four days. He went back to Rosemonde's to spend Christmas Eve.

She had put flowers on a tablecloth over two small tables pulled together, so that they would be more comfortable. The smell of good cooking filled the room.

"I imagine," she said, "that you couldn't care less about Christmas Eve parties and midnight mass. But in my case, in the fifteen years since my poor father died and the five my son's been travelling the world, this is actually the first time that I haven't been alone on the night before Christmas. Anyway, for what I'm about to tell you, I'd prefer you to have a bit to drink . . ."

She served him everything he liked. That is to say, things that are hard to digest and bad for the health: foie gras, a coulis of truffles with capers, a plump *demi-deuil* chicken.* They drank nothing but champagne that had lost its label – a present from a summer resident from Rheims – which had been lying in the cellar for four years. She had chilled it in the snow on the north side of the courtyard. "The cold in the fridge," she claimed, "makes it a bit harsh." "What a woman!" he said to himself, as he watched the magnificent, rhythmical sway of her hips as she came and went.

"And now," she announced, "before I go and turn out the crème caramel, I'd like to talk to you for a moment . . . You won't laugh at what I'm about to say, will you?"

"Oh!" Laviolette exclaimed. "You know how much I admire you. Would I do that?"

"It's not very nice . . . two women betraying a trust . . ."

Her eyes clouded over as she thought about it. Laviolette rolled a cigarette. Rather awkwardly, Rosemonde also began to smoke one –

* *Demi-deuil* means half-mourning, when white and a few muted colours may be worn as well as black. It refers to a method of cooking where strips of black truffles are inserted under the skin of the poultry, which is first blanched before being roasted. The bird is sometimes served with a white sauce that also contains truffles.

a filter-tip, of course. Then she nervously stubbed it out in the ashtray.

"A woman who listens at keyholes . . . that's not very nice either."

"Do you listen at keyholes?"

"I've done it twice. The other day when you were talking to your men in your room. And last night when you were talking to my customers. You were marvellous!"

"You surely don't want to speak to me about the hippies, do you Rosemonde?"

"Oh! You haven't had enough to drink."

"Rosemonde, if you want to speak to the Law, go right ahead and be frank. There are two men in me. The second can never be drunk. And besides, someone killed Brèdes, a dear friend of mine."

"Don't talk like that. You make me shiver. It's as though I'm seeing someone else in you."

"You see 'A stranger dressed in black, as like you as a brother.' Tell me what you know."

"What I suppose, more like! It's because I heard you speak of 'money worries'. I realised that you were trying to find out last night which of the seven needed a lot of money. Are you sure that it's one of them?"

"Ninety percent sure."

Rosemonde sighed.

"A customer who has killed seven people. Do you think that has no effect on me? I'm flabbergasted. I may even be sitting on the chair he usually has."

"Me too. Don't get worked up about that. Just tell me . . ."

"It didn't just dawn on me. I was thinking about it all night."

She sighed so deeply that each time the nipple of one breast rose under her blouse and pressed against her champagne flute.

"A man who needs a lot of money . . . What could that mean? A gambler? We'd know about it. Someone with a prodigal son? They all have model children in good jobs or about to be . . . A man with an extravagant wife? They all are, but they have no imagination, so that their spending doesn't go beyond their ability to pay. But take, for example, a man who has an affair that is costing him a fortune. A woman whose eyes are too big for her stomach. In another town? Mind you, if it's in another town, we'll never find out . . ."

"We'll find out all right," Laviolette said. "It may take time, but we'll know eventually."

"But – and this is what I thought – what if it was here?"

"Ah! If it was here, that would make things much easier."

"At about five this morning," Rosemonde said, "I may have had a glimmer. I wanted to go and wake you up . . . But, I have scruples about doing so. Pour me some champagne. I'm probably giving myself away . . ."

She drank three quarters of the glass.

"Mmm! That's so good! It just slips down your throat . . . I've mentioned Francine Morelon to you, haven't I?"

"Yes, the other night. Alyre's wife?"

"Who knows? She's a person who doesn't really love anyone, apart from men and her son, but for some reason she likes me. Anyway, whenever she has a discreet telephone call to make, she comes here. She gives me a knowing smile. She shakes my hand and says, "How are you?" as though we shared a heap of secrets. Sometimes I even wonder . . . she keeps my hand in hers for so long."

"OK. That's another matter," muttered Laviolette.

"Oh, it's just an impression . . . Anyway, on that day – my story's in two parts; that's what I was thinking about – anyway, the first time, maybe about a year and a half ago, she comes in dressed up as usual, with all her fancy jewellery (that's the important thing, her jewellery). Alyre is always admiring it. 'It's incredible how much Francine loves fancy jewellery. She'll ruin us with her fancy jewellery. She's got maybe 100,000 francs' worth.' 'Good Lord! A hundred thousand francs!' those around him exclaim. Then he shrugs his shoulders, 'Old currency, of course!' Now on that day – it was in August – there was a fellow at the bar. He was dirty, with a scruffy beard growing all around his neck, and the shorts he was wearing . . . well, my dear, they were so dirty they'd have stood up on their own! He was slowly drinking half a litre of beer, taking advantage of the shade. Francine makes her discreet telephone call, asks me how much she owes me, kisses me (which she never does normally), gives a come-hither look to the dirty guy at the counter, then leaves, swinging her behind . . . The fellow watches her go, gives a low whistle and turns to me. He says to me, 'That friend of yours certainly dresses well!' I don't know whether you've noticed, Superintendent, that I'm not too fond of anyone praising other merchandise than mine in my own establishment, or treating it as if it didn't exist . . . 'Why?' I said to him in a rather frosty voice. 'Why? Did you see her jewels?' 'Her jewels? They come from Fanta-Bijou, like mine.' 'I don't know where yours come from. I haven't seen them,' he said calmly, 'but I do know that hers are the real thing. The necklace isn't in the best taste or the very finest quality, but in a reputable jeweller's shop it can't have cost less than six grand, and if you said four for the diamond-set watch, you wouldn't be far wrong.' I felt as though I'd been hit on the head by the chiming clock. 'You're not really trying to tell me that Francine had 100,000 francs' worth of jewels on her today? Are you? And, if I may say so, what would *you* know about it?' 'Oh,' he said modestly, 'not a lot, but, well . . . When I'm wearing my morning coat, I'm the head salesman at Van Cleef.' Yes, that's what he says to me! Point blank, just like that! He throws his money for the beer on the counter, turns his back to me and walks off on his skinny legs with the wallet sticking out of the pocket of his dirty shorts."

"Are you saying, Rosemonde, that she didn't have the ring yet? Try to remember. When was that?"

"As I told you, in August last year. Almost eighteen months ago. But just a moment. In July this year, she came back . . ."

"Did she have the ring?"

"No. Not yet. But you'll see. She lifts the receiver – I'll cut a long story short – and she says, 'Have you got it?' I was in the kitchen, making a fair amount of noise with the pots and pans in case – heaven forbid! – she might be thinking that I was listening to her. But either she wasn't being careful enough or else my ears were too good. I could still hear,

'Good! Then have it ready and I'll call for it.' And after that, 'No! No! In four days' time, with the tractor. When I bring the lavender.' Now, what she said was not terribly important. What was important was the way she said it, and above all the fact that when she left she gave me fifty centimes, the price of a local call. Therefore, she had just called someone from around here . . . And so, gradually, when I was remembering all that last night, I thought that since you are looking for someone who needs a lot of money, I'd be surprised if the man from Banon who's involved with the woman in question was not a bit strapped for cash . . ."

Laviolette was up on his feet and making for the coat rack. He took down his overcoat and hat and the long muffler knitted by a former admirer who was absent-minded or thought him as tall as de Gaulle.

"But where are you going?" Rosemonde said, quite startled. "You haven't had the crème caramel. And your coffee. And the cigars I bought you."

"Afterwards!" Laviolette replied.

"After what?"

"After my own midnight mass!"

He had already wound the scarf three times around his neck. It was as constricting as an iron collar, and his voice seemed to come from deep inside it.

"Because, if I don't do something immediately, I can see your friend with a new piece of jewellery . . . a nice red necklace . . . blood-red!"

The *demi-deuil* goose was beginning to turn on the spit in the dining room hearth. The pristine white tablecloth had been brought out and laid with the best cutlery. The house was full of people: Alyre's mother, Francine's parents and her divorced sister, who was smoothing her skirt for the shepherd's benefit.

But the shepherd was sitting with his mouth open beside Alyre, watching Romy Schneider on TV delicately baring a little of her shoulder for Philippe Noiret in a panama hat.

Someone called out from below. Roseline, who had woken with a start, began making as much noise as the geese of the Capitol. The hunting dogs barked in the desperate hope of being let out. The goats in the shed shook the bells round their necks.*

"Who is it?" Alyre shouted through the half-open door, with one eye still on Romy Schneider's shoulder, which was already covered once more.

"Police!" Laviolette called.

The shepherd, with an instinctive guilty reaction, sprang to turn off the television.

Although he had just had a very good dinner, Laviolette was suddenly greeted by a mixture of such appetising smells when he opened the door that he could perhaps have sat down to eat again.

"Please don't stop what you're doing. Don't disturb yourselves. Don't worry. We'll just be in and out."

Everyone who had been involved with cooking the goose in the dining room had hurried to the kitchen door to see what was happening.

"Come in!" Alyre said. "Will you have something to drink?"

"No. Really. Is your wife there?"

"No," Alyre said. "She's gone out."

"Where has she gone?"

"Proserpine, do you know where she's gone?"

The sister who had been smoothing her skirt came towards the super-intendent, already looking worried, it seemed to him. Laviolette thought straight away that she was a sister with secrets, a knowing sister, one of those sisters in whom one confides. Her manner also said, "Speak to me".

She replied casually, "Well, she said she had one or two things to do and that afterwards, being deputy mayor, she had to go to midnight mass. She advised us to start cooking the goose at about ten o'clock . . . So, you see . . ."

"Come out here for a moment," Laviolette said.

He took her outside under the balcony, with no thought for her bare arms.

---

* These are the *menons*, neutered goats with bells around their necks, which lead the flocks of sheep on the *transhumance*: the annual journey to and from the summer pastures in the mountains of Provence.

"Your sister," he said quietly, "who gave her the jewellery she wears?"
She shivered, drew back, and was about to protest.

He immediately countered her objections.

"Her life depends on what you tell me."

"But I can't tell you. I don't know," the sister exclaimed in despair.
They both went back inside.

"This is no time to play games," Laviolette warned. "The murderer
has your wife in his sights, Alyre. If you know where she is, tell me
right now and we'll go there. She needs us . . . and she doesn't know
it," he added.

He wanted to spare people's susceptibilities and reputations. Alyre,
however, was quite oblivious to such details. He was pale, and the agitation he felt made the neck of his clean shirt flutter over his Adam's
apple.

"You don't know, Proserpine? You really don't know?"

"The only thing I know for certain is that she left on foot."

"Why on foot? She always take her car."

"I said that to her. She replied, 'I'm not going far, and besides, I need
to walk . . .'"

The old man standing by the kitchen door anxiously followed the
conversation, but didn't say a word. They must have been curtly told
for a long time now not to interfere, no matter what. The shepherd was
just as panic-stricken as Alyre. The thought of Francine's fifty-three
kilos out there on the road, at the mercy of anything and anyone, made
him overcome his usual restraint and step forward.

"Roseline!" he whispered.

"That's right! Alyre exclaimed. "Roseline will know. As soon as you
take her out, if there's a member of the household who isn't home yet,
she gets the scent and starts to look for them."

"Well, then, get her out right now!" Laviolette ordered.

He knew how incredibly quickly the killer could strike. He could still
hear him brushing past on the night Brèdes died; he could still see the
veil . . . He urged them on.

"Come on! Get your Roseline out here. There's not a moment to lose."

They all hurried over to the sty.

The gendarmes' van was waiting in front of the porch. Viaud had already got out when Alyre and the shepherd came back from the sty, pulled along by Roseline who was grunting and sniffing the wind.

The procession set off, headed by Roseline, searching from one rise to the next, pulling now Alyre, now the shepherd, in opposite directions at the end of her string. Behind them came the police van, driving slowly. In this way they crossed Banon, to the astonishment of people in the street going to friends' places for a party or to midnight mass.

"Hey, Alyre! All you all going to mass together?"

There were joyous cries from colleagues and drinking mates who had already been doing some serious celebrating to welcome the Redeemer.

"You haven't seen Francine, have you?"

"Ooh! I tell you, if we'd seen her, we'd have kept her with us!"

"Don't ask anything," the shepherd urged. "You know that Roseline . . ."

And indeed, Roseline took no notice of anyone or anything. She went along grunting, sometimes stopping so suddenly that Alyre and the shepherd had to hold on to her rump to stop themselves from falling over her.

The wide world lay there before them beneath the moonlight like a fabulous masterpiece. Roseline didn't hesitate. She charged on through the brambles, down the frozen ruts of a sunken road. It was a dirt road that had been cleared the day before by the Highways Department. They drove along slowly for several minutes between two banks of snow sometimes eighty centimetres high.

"I know where we're going!" Viaud cried.

"That's what I'm afraid of too," Laviolette murmured beside him.

"We won't need Roseline any longer . . . There's no fork in this road. It leads straight to the home of one of the suspects."

"I know," Laviolette said. "And I know which one. That's what worries me . . ."

"With good reason."

"No. You don't understand. An awful suspicion has just crossed my mind: what if Francine was just going to meet a lover? What do you think of that? If instead of arresting a killer, we stumbled on a case of adultery? And with the husband on our heels! What would you think of that, Chief?"

Viaud shook his head gravely.

"I don't think so. I sense something else. I don't feel it's a time for jokes. In any case, we can now dispense with the husband, the sow and the shepherd, since we know where we're going."

That was easier said than done. Neither the husband nor the shepherd, and definitely not Roseline the sow, would give up.

"All right! Bring them along," Laviolette said. "Too bad for them if they see something they won't like."

But the pig? Alyre and the shepherd would not hear of going back or leaving the sow tied to a tree. It took the six of them to get huge Roseline into the back of the van. They set off again at last, this time at a much higher speed.

Claire had been on tenterhooks all day. That morning, the slim, well-dressed inspector who was staying at the same hotel had once again sat down beside her in the foyer. He had been trying for two days to discreetly seduce her, and persuade her in every way he knew to spend two or three hours in a room with him which, he assured her, would have no further consequences for either of them. A man who has designs like these will always let slip something he would not otherwise mention, as he needs to make himself seem important.

"I won't have much time for the usual preliminaries," he told her. "We're about to arrest the killer. There are only five suspects left . . . Don't you think that you and I could hurry things up a little?"

What had she replied? "Don't count on it!" or some such silly remark.

In the afternoon she put Mambo on the lead and joined the rest of Banon roaming around the truffle woods under investigation. And now, she had just spotted Francine down below, crossing the square in her boots and cape, with her unmistakable walk. Where was she going? It was too early for mass, and besides, does a woman like Francine go to mass? And on foot! Except on one particular occasion, every time Claire had seen that woman during the whole time that she had been in Banon, Francine was shutting her car door . . .

All these signs indicated that the investigation was nearing a conclusion. She had to make up her mind . . . make up her mind . . . She felt overwhelmed by anxiety and the weight of her responsibilities. The factory . . . the whole affair . . . To have done so much, only to see it snatched away from you? No, it mustn't happen . . .

She slowly walked up and down the room in her expensive shoes and Saint-Laurent Boutique dress. Suddenly, her mind was made up. She went out of the room and, unnoticed, left the hotel. The clatter from the kitchens underscored the noise of the customers happily celebrating in the crowded restaurant. Going down the stairs, she was greeted by the admiring silence of the pimply kitchen hand, who stood to attention to let her pass.

The enormous Mercedes in the square stood sparkling and solid beside the drunkenly swaying pines. She got behind the wheel and buckled her seat belt.

XXIII

THE MAN LYING FULLY CLOTHED ON THE BED LET THE silence sweep over him. Soon he would be on the move, but in the meantime, until he calmly went to midnight mass as usual, he had to be invisible, lie low, keep away from other men; not have to speak, reply or smile.

Every ten minutes or so, the large bedroom that had been the scene of so much jubilation resounded like a drum to a soft, thundering sound that shook everything: walls, partitions, ceiling. A wave from some mysterious upheaval seemed to go right through the house. It felt like falling into an air pocket. At each warning sign, you thought, "The house will go this time for sure!" But no, it didn't. Yet you had to be really familiar with the phenomenon not to think that every time. The man gave a silent laugh at the thought of all those women – thin, fat, dark or fair – who had suddenly torn themselves away from him and run naked for the door at this violent manifestation of fate. "It's the house, silly! Come back to bed."

It was indeed the house. It was curiously curved like a crescent moon and the roofs followed the line in a sickle shape. Three hundred years ago the Friars Minor had built this house on a developing sinkhole, either through ignorance or wanting to tempt the Lord or impose an additional penance on themselves. The ground there is like a fermenting Gruyère cheese. Sometimes it bursts like dough that's too rich, splitting into a fine, deep hole. Ancient waters whispering their way between the sky and the sea glisten a long way down on the bottom. The buildings had been restabilised as far as possible over the years at the whim of this bizarre geological phenomenon. The earth had not moved for more than a hundred years now, but they had never been able to avoid that noise like the string of a double-bass being plucked, that sudden reminder of the earth's elasticity, which came at regular intervals from the abyss below. The man lying on the bed dressed in his Sunday best had been born amid these jolts from the ground below. He had grown up with them, married with them. Now he was alone. His wife had taken their child to her parents at Saint-Michel-l'Observatoire. "I could even get used to you," she said. "I'm tough. But I'll never get used to your house."

The man was breathing very quietly. He had to lie low. He was hopeful, but afraid. Yes, he was scared, but he still had an erection. Francine! He only had to picture her in his mind to find himself in this state. He sighed. It had been so long since the last time . . . And before the next time, he still had to find another 5000 francs to make up the amount for the diamond brooch she needed to grant him a rendezvous . . . There was the truffle season, which had been so much better than expected . . . Unfortunately, he would not get the full benefit from it until next year, and before that he would have to treat a lot more trees . . . But afterwards . . . He could shower Francine with those jewels she wanted so much. And besides, he wouldn't need them any more, for by that time she would love him for himself. All it would take was just one more meeting. He thought of all the things he would do for her. He would be so good, he would be so inventive that she would have an orgasm at last. Yes . . . He would feel her whole body quiver as she came. That's what he was striving for. He used all his strength and all his skill against this block of marble; the arm she kept over her eyes the whole time; the limp, unresponsive body, as silent as a closed book. God Almighty! It was unbelievable! He clenched his fists. Even his cock rebelled, as if he had put it through a tight iron ring.

The house was drawing its elastic breath. He felt himself swaying as in a hammock. The sound of small fists knocking on the door came from down below. Two quick knocks followed by two slow ones. He didn't move. He mustn't give in to temptation. Not this evening. Maybe never again . . . That was his fear talking, the fear of being irresistibly lured on, only to wake one morning at dawn facing the guillotine. He longed for midnight, for the bell to ring in the steeple. It seemed to him that the church should protect him. His childhood faith still burned in him like a candle, in that body lost to the world. It grieved him that now he could never go to confession again . . .

The knocking at the door down below became more insistent, its agreed pattern giving way to what sounded like panic . . . Pebbles were being thrown up hard against the shutters. He didn't move. A furious, guttural voice he didn't recognise cursed him, the house, the whole country. Another voice joined in. He could hear hard leather-soled sandals slapping over the flagstones in the courtyard. Two poor young creatures with wild hair, clasping each other in frustration, went off down the path to Montsalier.

He cursed that invisible trail, the source of all his misfortunes. In the beginning, they asked for wine, cheese or potatoes. They paid. One day they laughingly brought up the subject of hash and the fact that they could pay for it. They left a packet of seeds on the corner of the table, as if they had forgotten it. This was just at the time when he was having trouble filling the hole that Francine's expensive tastes were making in his budget. And so one thing led to another . . . The hardest thing, before, was to resist the girls. They were always short of money to buy their pot, so they offered themselves. He refused. It was the highest proof of his love for Francine. He kept the precious cigarettes for those who were solvent; the others . . . He endured the sight of these girls who knowingly revealed parts of their often superb bodies under their ragged clothes. He endured seeing them fondle themselves in front of him in the hope that he would give in and give them the drug free or almost. But no! He was keeping himself for Francine. The girls would leave him, distraught and dishevelled, hurling insults as they went.

He must have dozed off for two minutes. A familiar soft metallic sound woke him up. Someone was feeling for the key under the stone fossil next to the door. He leaped to the window. In the moonlight he could see the back of a caped figure walking quickly and lightly towards the porch; someone at once familiar and strange; someone in soft leather boots. He was going to call out, then changed his mind. He silently went down the stone staircase.

The main room was lighter than usual on those nights. He had built up the fire for Christmas. The incandescent glow from the slow-burning logs shone on the walnut table where a little mound of light reflected star-like shimmers over the pendulum in the clock. He went over to it without knowing what it was, and it was only when he laid his hand on that cold light that the truth dawned on him.

He opened the door. There was Francine a hundred metres away running off down the beech tree path. He thought of calling her, keeping her with him, perhaps even taking advantage of the opportunity. But the little heap in the palm of his hand was as cold as a corpse. It was all there: the ring, the necklace, the diamond-set watch. The silence in his soul was so deep that he felt he could hear the tick-tock of the watch beating in his hand. As he thought what this meant, he felt his life collapsing around him, like crumbling stone walls.

If the jewels no longer had any power over Francine, there would no longer be any hope of having her in his bed, all to himself for a whole night. There would be no time to find the secret of her orgasm, to master her ever-changing, fleeting, determinedly hidden erogenous zones . . . Two things became clear at the same time: that he would never have her again, and that she represented a mortal danger to him. She was the ideal witness . . .

He threw the jewels against the farm wall. The house gave one of its pulsations from the depths, echoing his action. In his rage, he was tempted at first to give chase and strangle her. But the careful trapper's instinct still lingered there beneath his wounded pride. It only took a moment to think of a radical means of killing her without arousing suspicion. When he was looking through the blinds a moment ago, he had noticed Francine stumbling in her fine boots. Yesterday morning the Highways Department had cleared the access road, but there was still a steep 60–80 cm wall of snow on each side. In what she was wearing, Francine could not easily get over that barrier, and if she did, it would be easy to catch up with her on foot. But he wouldn't let her get over it. He'd chase after her in the car, speeding up, slowing down, braking suddenly. By the time she understood why he didn't catch up or run her over, it would be too late. She would run out of breath and die, her heart bursting under the strain. He would provide her with the first opportunity to show that she had one . . .

He started up the engine of his 4 CV. The thin cruel smile was there on his face once more.

The moon was sweeping its light over the Lure mountains. It played with a swift cloud that swirled it around, spat it out of its coils, and finally detached itself, leaving the moon to reign supreme in the sky, where it dimmed the stars.

In that bright light, the gendarmes' van, its headlamps switched off, reached the top of the Doline, which dominated the Friars' land. A light was on there. You could just make out the silhouette of the house through the beech trees. Now sparse, now suddenly massed, they partly hid it from view in the stark tangle of their winter branches.

The house was reached by three very large hairpin bends, clearly delineated by the monks of old on the sides of the huge sinkhole. They had recently been cleared by the bulldozer. The Highways Department had been through the morning before, leaving a bank of snow 60 cms high, and twice that height in the bends which outlined the route. The distillery hollow, on the other hand, which cut the road at a right angle, shone with hard ice. Further up the road, a light-coloured car could be seen in the moonlight standing close against the galvanised-iron side of the shed.

"Some old wreck," Laviolette thought.

The tall trees shivered in response to something known only to themselves.

Chief Viaud, the two gendarmes, Alyre and the shepherd got out of the van that was still being shaken by Roseline turning round and round inside. They all stood still on the edge of the Doline, like staff officers looking down on a battlefield.

"A battlefield of love," Laviolette thought. "That Francine has come to see her lover in secret and spend Christmas with him . . . The fact that she didn't want to use her car was proof enough that she didn't want to be seen. And here I am, like an idiot, following a sow screaming blue murder! Blue murder! For God's sake!"

It was then that everything became clear to him; the sinister truth stared him in the face. He clapped his hand over his mouth to stifle his horror.

"What's up?" Viaud said.

"What's up is that I'm bloody stupid! That for the last week that sow has been telling me who the murderer is and I haven't understood her! That Francine's life is in real danger!"

"Look!" cried Viaud.

In the distance, near the farm, a woman who looked like a black ant against the white ground was running out into the open along the straight line before the three sharp bends. Sometimes she tried to get over the bank to escape into the open fields, but slipped on the icy snow. A 4 CV was chasing her less than ten metres behind. All its lights were out as it jolted along at reduced speed, its engine labouring and its nightmarish chains grinding on road.

"Francine!" Alyre screamed.

He and the shepherd, followed by two gendarmes, rushed through the snow towards the slight figure running for its life. She was too far away to hear them. She was too far away for them to help her. Then she fell. The 4 CV rushed at her, nearly touching her, still making as much noise as possible.

"He'll make her heart give out!" thought Laviolette. "She'll be dead before we can get to her! God! What a bloody fool I am!"

Francine got up and started running once again, looking a little uncoordinated, a little disorientated. The 4 CV roared behind her, surging forward . . . braking . . . surging forward . . . braking . . .

Standing on the top of the Doline, Laviolette could only feel how helpless he was, while Viaud phoned orders to his men:

"As soon as you're within range, shoot at his tyres."

"They'll never get there in time," Laviolette said.

Behind them in the van, Roseline was giving ear-piercing shrieks as she tried to kick down the walls. Laviolette had a sudden inspiration. He went around to the back of the van and released the sow, who nearly knocked him down. Roseline immediately made a beeline for the black figure more than 500 metres below who was stumbling in front of the 4 CV, literally pushing her forward. Roseline was now bellowing real war cries.

"Look!" Laviolette shouted.

He was pointing further away at the car against the distillery wall that he had mistaken for a wreck. It was also starting up with no lights. It slid down the icy hollow in a wild slalom that sent it from one rut to another. At the spot where the rough ravine met the main road, it stopped suddenly.

"It's Claire's Mercedes!" Laviolette exclaimed.

"What's she doing?" Viaud asked.

Running, stumbling, Francine passed the car lying in ambush beneath the trees without noticing it. The 4 CV ten metres behind her also passed it. Then the Mercedes moved off again, joining the road behind the 4 CV. Suddenly its four lights and fog lamps lit up on full beam. She accelerated and caught up with the 4 CV. On the top of the Doline, Laviolette and Viaud heard a dull thud. The 4 CV, thrown from one snow wall to the other, zigzagged, then righted itself with engine roaring as it tried to escape. But the Mercedes was already hitting it again, harder this time. The little car dived on its shock absorbers and stopped. The Mercedes backed for ten metres, revved, and drove full speed at the obstacle in its path.

Francine had lengthened the distance between herself and her pursuer by twenty metres during that stop. She fell, and remained stretched out on the road. She felt warm breath on her that seemed to come from loud, hot panting. Roseline lay down against her body, on the side where danger threatened.

The unforgettable crack of the crushed bodywork echoed in the night. It was the Mercedes ramming the 4 CV, sending it into the snow, backing, coming at it again in growling first gear. The Mercedes swept the light vehicle and the snow wall before it like a tank. It pushed its prey forward for three metres, then finally jammed it against the trunk of a huge beech tree, which shuddered to the ends of its branches.

"Shoot at the tyres!" yelled Viaud.

Four shots were heard one after the other. The Mercedes came to a stop on its wheel rims.

Alyre and the shepherd fell breathless on Francine's body. Alyre put his arms around her legs; the trembling shepherd felt her heart under her bra. It was a moment he would never forget . . .

"She's alive!" he shouted to Alyre. "She's alive!"

"And Roseline?" Alyre asked.

She raised her head and licked his face to show him that she was holding out.

There they were, the three of them – Roseline, Alyre, and the shepherd – in a tight circle around the apple of their eye.

Viaud and Laviolette rushed down the bends; the gendarmes ran to the Mercedes. The night was silent again, apart from the feeble moans of a man who thought he was screaming. They managed to get him out of the shattered 4 CV and lay him on the snow.

His wild womaniser's face was still as extraordinarily handsome to behold in the moonlight as always. He took ten minutes to die, cradled in his broken bones. He thought he cried out three times as he tried to raise himself.

"A priest! I want a priest!"

But what came out was no more than a murmur. Laviolette was the only one to hear him. As he held him in death, he thought of Brèdes' bleeding artery. But it was no consolation.

Quite unhurt, Claire Piochet undid her seat belt, got out of the Mercedes and came to watch her victim die, anxious to see the lips still moving.

"I told you, Superintendent, that I'd get there before you . . ."

Laviolette did not answer straight away. First he closed the eyes of Albert Pipeau, the man who had women galore. Pipeau the flute player, who would never play again.

He got up slowly. He looked into Claire's face, into her eyes that you'd have to be mad not to fall in love with.

"Claire," he said, "I'm arresting you for the murder of Albert Pipeau, but also of your brother, Jeremy Piochet."

"You'll find that hard to prove!" she replied as calm as could be.

"Don't worry. I'll manage to convince a jury. You have a very good motive, and you've made several mistakes. OK, put the cuffs on her! She's serious enough for that!"

"I want a lawyer!" Claire demanded.

"Whatever you like!" Laviolette said. "But it's Christmas Eve. We'll talk about that later."

The church bell in the village was calling the faithful to mass. One of the gendarmes had hurriedly sent a message ordering a car for Albert. They all slowly started on their way back to the van. Roseline was so overcome by human evil that her snout trailed in the snow. You felt that she preferred to be a sow. They heaved her once again into the wagon.

Francine's breathing slowly grew softer. Everyone, sitting slumped on their seats, also got their breath back. Claire looked at her wrists in the steel bracelets. Francine stared at her for a moment.

"Alyre," she said suddenly, "hold my hand! I think I should talk now!" And talk she did.

XXIV

"ROSEMONDE!" LAVIOLETTE SAID. "CLOSE THE DOOR. I'M GOING to tell you a love story! You deserve to hear it. They're waiting for me at the police station for a press conference, but you have priority . . ."

His suitcase and his blue sailor's bag were already on the seat beside him. He rolled himself a cigarette.

"You see, Rosemonde, Albert Pipeau, that man who had women galore, all he wanted was one woman, and she didn't want him."

"Francine."

Rosemonde slapped her thigh.

"That's the second time I feel as if I've been hit on the head by Big Ben!"

She looked thoughtful for a moment or two.

"The handsomest man for thirty kilometres around and the hottest woman in the whole district . . . Well then . . . She wasn't being hypocritical?"

"What do you mean?"

"When she claimed that she couldn't stand the touch of his skin; that this fine lady couldn't bear him to come within three metres of her! She said it all the time, and I thought to myself, 'She does carry on! People will notice.' I could hardly believe my ears, and yet there were things that I saw myself. When we were at a party or a dance, and they were sometimes close to each other, as people who've known each other since childhood often are, he would sometimes put his hand on her shoulder. Well! You should have seen her almost collapse under its weight, move her shoulder away as if his touch had dirtied it. Her whole being cringed, like . . ." Rosemonde said, searching for a comparison, "a snail's horns, when you accidentally touch them."

"She shrank . . ."

"That's it! She shrank from him. She shrank. I could sense it. She would have shrunk into a ball, if she could. Like a hedgehog."

"She'd have shrunk to the core . . ." Laviolette said.

"That's right. To the core. So, it was true after all. She wasn't being hypocritical. It was true. I should have suspected that she couldn't be such a good actress."

"What do you expect, my dear Rosemonde, after what Francine told us with a wealth of unbelievable detail – I think the shock she had just experienced must have intoxicated her like champagne. It seems that his was the only skin that gave her the creeps. 'Skin that had the same effect on me as a snake's,' she said."

"Albert!" Rosemonde exclaimed in disbelief. "Hippies, peasants, ladies, young, not so young, holiday-makers, Parisiennes; the mistress of the general in charge of the base; some I can't name . . . One night when I couldn't sleep, I added them up – and that's only the ones I knew. He must have had a hundred and fifty!"

She thought for a few moments.

"And why not take it when it's offered."

"Yes," Laviolette continued. "A hundred and fifty, but not Francine! Mind you, it didn't worry him in the beginning. She wasn't in the fore-front of the women he had in his sights."

"That's true," Rosemonde said. "She doesn't stand out. It's after paying some attention to her that the men begin to think, 'Well, well . . .'"

"He'd promised himself that he could have her when he wanted to. 'She's playing at being distant, but I'll only have to hold her . . .' Or whatever men think in that situation . . ."

"But . . . Excuse me for interrupting you . . . Am I right in thinking that she said all this in front of Alyre?"

"Yes indeed! It came out quite naturally."

"But how did Alyre take it?"

"Good as gold! He kept on holding her hand and gazing into her eyes. You see, he'd nearly lost her."

Rosemonde rolled her eyes and clapped her hands together.

"And then one day Albert thought the time was right. It was in August, when Francine was taking the lavender to the distillery. Did you know that she drives the tractor? She told me, 'I was hot and sweaty, with bits of lavender all over me. I was just wearing a dirty blouse and a bra that wasn't much better. Albert was alone. I was getting the lavender flowers that were annoying me out of my bra with a handkerchief. I do admit that I was wrong . . .' Pretending to help her get down from the tractor, he lifted her up and without any warning held her tight against him. Straight away he started feeling for her private parts with his hand and the rest. She gave no warning either. She raised her knee and jabbed him where it hurts, which made him let go immediately. She ran to the distillery, where a poker was glowing red-hot in the hearth. She grabbed it and said to him, 'If you try to lay a hand on me, I promise you I'll make a cross with this on your face. No-one will ever look at you again!'"

"She was going a bit far."

"That's what I tried to tell her, but she said, 'Well, would you go to bed with a snake?' And do you think he took that as the end of the matter? He took it as a sudden outburst. Maybe she had her period. He believed anything rather than the truth. I'll make a long story short. One thing led to another and she begins to fill his thoughts. He sleeps around, but half-heartedly . . . You know what I mean. He watches her. Alyre often talks proudly about his wife's fancy jewellery. He's forever saying how wonderful Francine is. One day at a fair, Albert buys about 500 francs' worth of fancy jewellery. He tries the gentle approach. 'There was at least half a kilo of it,' Francine said. She laughs in his face."

Laviolette lit his cigarette and continued.

"Things get worse. The thought of Francine goes around and around in his brain. When he wakes at night in that creaking house, instead of thinking about any of his hundred and fifty real memories, he chooses one that's an illusion. He begins to blush when he meets her. He begins to experience embarrassing failures in his nights of love – he actually told Francine about it. We know the date when he withdrew 50,000 francs from the bank; the date when he bought the watch from a jeweller in the Rue de Rome in Marseilles. When did he open the box and dazzle Francine with it? Women who like jewellery know immediately when it's the real thing, even if they've never had any. From that moment there are two insomniacs in Banon: Albert can't sleep because of Francine, and Francine can't sleep because of the watch. 'After all . . . No, it's impossible! No, I couldn't! It's a fabulous watch.' I'm telling you this in just a few words, but the account of her shilly-shallying takes up a full page of the report. Three months, it took! Three months later, she phones him, 'Tuesday at ten o'clock, Rue Sylvabelle, if you bring the watch.'"

He broke off to roll another cigarette and take a deep breath.

"And it's here, Rosemonde, that the love story begins, as Albert, ever optimistic, tells himself that she'll be rolling at his feet in five seconds flat. 'I can tell you,' Francine said, 'that if I hadn't been holding the watch in my fist, it would have killed me, I hated it so much! I spent a whole week trying to wash it out of my mind. I dared not touch my own skin! I kept my hand away from my body, so that I would not touch it. I swore I'd never do it again.' She was like a sack of walnuts in Albert's arms. He's absolutely stunned. Six months later it's the necklace. Eight months later, Francine sacrifices herself again. Once again it's the limp sack of walnuts. What can you do? When two skins, two bodies don't match, you can put God the Father between them, but it won't be reversed! And Albert's skin revolted Francine's . . ."

"To think that there were so many others who lusted after him . . . and he never even looked at them."

"That's the way it is, my dear Rosemonde. As Molière says, 'The world, dear Agnes, is a strange place.' Anyway, this is the time when

Albert starts planting cannabis here and there on his property, as he is having great difficulty filling the hole in his bank account. There are payments to be made to the Crédit Agricole. Lavender is not selling well. The National Office has just withdrawn 200 tons . . . The honey is dark because the bees have gathered too much pollen from oak tree flowers. The Marseilles people won't buy it. Meanwhile, he becomes more and more obsessed with Francine. It's basically the Pygmalion story over again: someone who wants to bring a statue to life."

"I understand," Rosemonde said.

"He can think of nothing but the next time he'll make love to her. He starts to bet on the horses, take lottery tickets. He says to himself, 'You'll see. It'll work next time. It must work.'"

"How do you know that's what he thinks?"

"My dear Rosemonde," he said, running the end of the cigarette paper across his tongue, "there's not one man in a hundred who hasn't thought it about a woman some time or another. And so, he keeps looking forward to that day. He takes another 60,000 francs out of his bank account three months before a bill is due and that money has been set aside to cover it. Off he goes to Marseilles to buy the ring."

"What a bitch!" Rosemonde said under her breath.

"In May they meet again in the Rue Sylvabelle for the third and last time. With the same negative result, as the scientists say. I don't know if you realise that during this time, Albert has literally ruined himself. He has to take out the first mortgage he's ever had on his property. The truffle season has been catastrophic and Francine is now like a cancer growing inside his head.

"A real bitch!" Rosemonde said again.

"That's when Albert, who fought in Algeria, is invited by my friend Brèdes to a war veterans' reunion. They've all drunk a bit, the weather's bad, and there's not much to do. They wander from room to room. Someone notices a book on the lectern and starts leafing through it . . . I suppose Brèdes must have seen it. He comes over. I suppose he says to them . . . I can almost hear him," Laviolette says sadly. "Relaxed, a bit lord of the manor – you can say it now that he's dead . . . 'You're looking at the book. As a matter of fact, there's something in it to interest truffle hunters! Just a moment. It's very amusing. I'll read it to you.' And this is what he read."

Laviolette took the dirty brown volume out of his pocket.

"I'll have to translate it for you, because it's in old French, but here's what it means . . ."

He opened the book.

"*A formula for obtaining a profusion of truffles by sprinkling the truffle trees with human blood.*"

"That's horrible!" Rosemonde exclaimed.

"*If you obtain several pints of human blood,*" continued the imperturbable Laviolette, "*and spread it over the truffle woods, you will find that you have the most marvellous harvest that ever was. The monks of Yeusefilt relate it in their chronicle. At one time, a large party of peasants was surrounded by the counts in the said Yeusefilt truffle woods, and there was such slaughter that the monks whose task it was to bury them sank into the blood that soaked the earth as after driving rain. And the next year such a profuse harvest as never was seen. The counts of Taillerang, who lived in Périgord at that time, adopted the custom each time to do such slaughter of peasants in their truffle woods, and were well pleased.*"

"Good Lord!" Rosemonde whispered. "It can't be true. He couldn't have been as crazy as that."

"Wait. I'll skip over two pages of horrors to be considered by anyone who wants to try the method . . ."

He continued reading.

"*But as he does it, the beneficiary of this knowledge must always take care not to have commerce with the Black Angel, and during the task should protect himself from him with some appropriate contrivance . . .*"

Laviolette picked up a neatly wrapped and numbered parcel beside him. "Exhibit no. 12.'" He carefully took out something light and airy which he spread out in front of Rosemonde, then moved this way and that on his fist like a marionette. It was the black straw hat with its funereal spotted veil.

"Good Lord!" Rosemonde whispered again. "It's the *Uillaoude*'s *mourrail* – her spell-caster's black veil. To think that my poor mother confided in her, trusted her. Thirty years on, it still makes my blood run cold."

"That was it, the 'appropriate contrivance'. While he watered his truffle trees with his victims' blood, he protected himself from the devil with it. It took us a long time to find it on his property: he'd hung it on the chain down the well, half-way between the rim and the surface of the water twenty metres below. With the knife. Alyre told me subsequently that he'd seen this *mourrail* on the evening when his sow was attacked. She must have surprised Albert working on one of his victims. All he could do as this 180-kilo pig rushed at him in the dark was to drop everything and defend himself by throwing stones. If only Alyre had told me about it earlier . . ."

"Good Lord!" Rosemonde groaned. "How could such horrible ideas still exist in a man's head?"

"When a person is completely under the spell of an obsession, anything is possible. Albert listens to it all and laughs like the rest of them, but he's none too bright and, besides, don't forget that he's one of the *Uillaoude*'s nephews. He absorbed the paranormal with his mother's milk, with the magic words. He's well-dressed, has a good car, women galore, but beneath all that, inside he has a really warped mind. And so, he pinches the book. Perhaps to look for some other formula. And don't forget that during this time his hippie clientele for cannabis is increasing. Business is good! Who would suspect it's being grown by Albert Pipeau down there in the quiet depths of the Banon countryside? They come in the evening; they smoke; they drink a bit. They sprawl on the ground; they get sleepy. Albert reads the fateful passage again. Soon he knows it by heart. He remembers that his family have always been pig slaughterers, from father to son. Hanging from an iron beam among the joists in the stable, there is still that enormous S-hook that was used to hang the pig before it was eviscerated. He also looks at the enormous key to the Protestant tomb hanging on the nail with the Post Office calendar. The calendar is thrown out every year and the key is automatically put back over it, since who knows when. It's been

196

there for generations. It has a label attached. No-one knows why it's there. '*Such a profuse harvest as never was seen,*' Albert recites to himself. He needs a million for the diamond brooch to give Francine . . . Who knows? If I had such a huge truffle harvest . . . And the extraordinary idea grows in his mind. 'What if I tried?' And, one night . . ."

"Please . . ." Rosemonde groaned, hiding her face.

"I'll make it short to save your feelings . . . But I can see him, see him with his rattling 4 CV, out at night with the body hidden under a sack on the back seat, going to put it in the Protestant tomb; and the bucket of blood mixed with sand beside him, going to spread it in his truffle woods. It's been proved conclusively: analyses of samples taken have shown large traces of human blood under seven different trees. One even matched the blood group of a victim. Perhaps Albert might have had his fourth night with Francine if he hadn't been stuck in the square at Banon on the night of the car accident. But also perhaps, if amongst all these murders, which do have a poetic quality, there hadn't been a genuine, sordid one committed for a perfectly plausible motive – one the public likes, a perfectly proper one: a murder committed for money. How did Claire know Albert? She's not talking. The charges against her are slender. But I think that the Department of Public Prosecutions will get her. She's been traced to Banon twice during the last six months. She must have followed her brother, tried to persuade him, beg him to come home.

"Why? What did he want to do?"

"Jeremy Piochet died because of the article in the Civil Code that says, 'No-one is obliged to remain in joint ownership'. His mother died six months ago. She left 20,000,000 new francs* represented by a plastic factory in the Ain *département*. As it happened, Jeremy was sick of the factory and sick of society. He liked his mates, wandering the road, freedom, ideas, lots of girls. *But*, as the autopsy will show, he didn't smoke pot. The family lawyer told us that he wanted to give his share to hippie communities. Now, it was the factory that was worth the

* Approximately £2,000,000.

197

20,000,000. Another group makes an offer to buy it. Jeremy wants to sell, and Jeremy is not obliged to remain in joint ownership. For Claire, who is an industrial chemist, the factory is her whole life, and Jeremy is a threat to this life, as his sister hasn't enough money to buy his share. When and how did she kill him? Was it in anger? Was it premeditated? Whatever the answer, she killed Albert to stop him from talking, so they must have know each other, they must have been in league. I'm saying that Albert could perhaps have got away with it; that he could still have gone on fertilising his truffle trees for quite some time. Yes, it's possible, but there was Jeremy's dog! The dachshund that was always with him, that didn't know his sister, and which she probably abandoned after the murder. The dachshund looks for its master. The dachshund comes across the Protestant tomb no-one bothered about because of the thickly growing trees that have hidden it for so long that no-one remembers it. I ask you, what finer place than a tomb for hiding bodies? Who would ever think of a tomb? Not a soul! Apart from the incomparable Roseline who has been balking for ages when she comes to that thicket of laurels. That Roseline . . . I'm going to have my photo taken beside her before I leave. She's been the real bloodhound on this case."

He paused for a moment, then continued.

"Claire made four mistakes. She should have got rid of the dog. Jeremy had to be killed with the same weapon that Albert used, and in the same way he used it. The fact that she failed to do it pleads in her favour: no doubt the murder was not premeditated, and it's likely that she didn't know about Albert's methods; therefore she wasn't his accomplice in the other murders. Secondly, the body wasn't lined up in the same way as the rest. It wasn't placed in chronological order – an order that Albert had followed strictly. Heaven knows for what reason. Thirdly, she should have got rid of the murder weapon. We found it in the boot of the Mercedes. As we suspected, it was a spanner, which Claire had very carefully cleaned and washed. But the electron microscope is like Lady Macbeth's remorse: with that, everything is eventually revealed. It's also thanks to the microscope that we detected Claire's fourth mistake.

On the night of the murder, she caught her coat on the thistles growing in the garden around the tomb. She left behind a tiny piece of the material. Oh, Rosemonde! I tell you, it was no bigger than a gossamer thread, but it was identical to those in the coat we found in her room when we searched it. And Rosemonde, that coat – there are only a hundred people in France who have one at the moment, because we counted them, and none of those people was anywhere near the Protestant tomb when Jeremy Piochet was taken there. That wraps it up!"

He gave a deep sigh and went on.

"As for me, my dear Rosemonde, I should resign from the force because my friend Brèdes died, and it's my fault . . ."

"How could it be your fault?"

"Yes, it is. Because on the morning of the day I was going to have lunch with the Marquis, I walked across the square when they were playing boules and Alyre Morelon had just arrived with his pig Roseline. Roseline was crying blue murder, and do you know who she was crying blue murder at, as she backed away, pulling on her lead? Well, it was Albert Pipeau! I can see it now. I shook his hand and I could see in his eyes that he was terrified! Because, you see, Albert's family are pig slaughterers from father to son. The pigs sense it. When the man comes to kill your pig, you have to hide him from the animal. It's because she saw one that Roseline began to cry blue murder. That should have tipped me off, afterwards when I thought about it again."

He got up. He'd told her just about everything. Poor Mambo sitting on the seat was waiting patiently for his fate to be decided.

"What are you going to do with him?" Rosemonde asked.

"Oh! I have a kind of refuge at Piégut, where there are already eight others. A retired game warden looks after them for me. He won't be unhappy there."

"Let me have him as a souvenir," Rosemond said.

"Why as a souvenir? Even policemen get holidays . . . And I'm not persona non grata in Banon."

"Certainly not in this place . . . Oh, I'm quite overcome by the whole story. Do you really think that is the reason Albert killed so many people? Do you think he was mad enough to believe the rubbish in those books for witches?"

"Well, what reason would you give?"

"Loneliness," Rosemonde replied.

That was all she said on the subject.

On the last market day in December, New Year's Eve, the *Uillaoude*, labouring with two heavy baskets of truffles while others had scarcely a kilo a day, suddenly appeared at the dealer's table. The circle of people around her miraculously widened.

"Are they your nephew's, *Uillaoude*?"

"Do you expect me to let them go to waste? The property comes to me. I have a mortgage on it. And there's more than your priest could bless!"

"Well, if it's all the same to you, take them to the market in Apt, will you?"

She shrugged.

"I was just doing you a favour. I got eight kilos a day. All of them 80–100 grams, and as round as your fist. They're truffles for Arab emirs, I tell you! And just smell them. Just breathe in that smell!"

But he recoiled in horror, as if the *Uillaoude* was about to force him to eat one. His lips drew back over his gold teeth.

"Oh, all right then!" she said, all commiseration. "I'll take up my old profession again. Since you still think you've been bewitched. When I think that big fellows like you could possibly believe that story!"

"But the police . . ."

"The police! Do *you* believe the police? I'll tell you what: these murders are another CIA job. And they killed my nephew, heaven help us, to stop him from talking!"

In the end, it was this version of the facts that would prevail in Banon.

The shepherd caught sight of his last ghost for the evening in the pendulum of the clock and watched it until it reached the plug hole in the sink. Down it went.

"I'm going to leave you," he announced, "but I'll come back again . . . I've thought about it, and I'm going to finish Law. Then I'll buy Maître Lagardère's practice in Banon. He's getting old. I'll be a solicitor like my father because all things considered, the liberal professions . . ."

Francine, who was putting the dishes away in the sideboard, stopped with her arms still raised when she heard this. Turning towards the shepherd, she tried to imagine him well-dressed in a shirt and tie, with a signet ring, nice fingernails and a good haircut.

"Oh! Really?" Alyre said.

He was ill at ease. He felt something was missing. His wife with her bare throat and no pearl necklace, her bare arm without a bracelet, her bare fingers with only an ordinary wedding ring . . . His wife looked poor and that made his heart ache.

When the shepherd had left the room, he turned to her.

"Tell me, Francine . . . Come to think of it, those 300,000 francs we have in the Savings Bank or treasury bonds . . . And those few gold coins in a bag hanging under Roseline's manger . . . What do you say to converting them into jewellery? After all, diamonds last . . . They increase in value . . . If ever there's a revolution . . ."

Francine suddenly turned round to face him. There were tears in her eyes.

"Do you know something, Alyre? I do love you!"

He turned away and went out into the yard. He walked over to Roseline's sty, where she was grunting softly, waiting for him to come and say goodnight.

Alyre was as happy as a king.